The
Golden Treasury
of
Selected School Works

Spike Potter

The Golden Treasury of Selected School Works

ISBN: 979-8421598558

Second Edition

This is a work of fiction. All the names, characters, businesses, places, events and incidents in this book are either the product of the author's imagination or used in a fictitious manner. Any resemblance to actual persons, living or dead, or actual events is purely coincidental.

To order more copies of this book or

for information about other books available, please visit:

www.lamplightpress.net

CONTENTS

"It is of the very essence and nature of this current work, here presented, to make something out of nothing, by whatever means present themselves to my imagination. I make no apology for the apparent, and probably actual, inanity of the discussions; let those who like them read them, and those who do not, turn elsewhere for their distractions."

A Wise Man

Foreword

As a reader, I do not care for lengthy introductions. Saying much more than they have need of saying, stating that which to all but idiots is obvious, taking space for the very sake of taking it, they so rudely disrupt the continuity of things – for, standing like some great, obscene, literary Cerberus, the prolix foreword deters the time-conscious reader from ever venturing into the book which it prefaces.

Let it be sufficient for me to say, then, that there follows a collection of prose school works, suitably – or unsuitably, depending upon one's point of view, accompanied by interviews with their respective authors.

For the sake of clarity, all, bar one, of the chapters follow strictly to a set pattern: a brief introduction, first part of interview, the school work, the teacher's comment, second part of interview, second school work (if applicable) et cetera.

Where the teacher has made comment other than final, that comment is highlighted within the text of the school work by parenthesized bold type. The school works have been set down exactly as their respective authors wrote them – spelling, grammatical and other errors entirely uncorrected.

For the benefit of *younger* readers, I should point out that "O Level" was the predecessor of what is now "GCSE"; to all intents and purposes the two are exactly the same thing.

In all cases, the identities of my interlocutors are protected by use of their first names only.

Spike Potter

On a boat, somewhere in an Ocean – I don't know where… but it's raining.

CHAPTER 1: CONCERNING 'THE DEATH OF CUCHULAIN'

Introduction

A few days after I placed an advertisement in a local newspaper asking for someone to send me a copy of an essay which they had written for their mock O Level/GSCE exam years ago, I received a reply from Oliver who had written an essay entitled *CONCERNING 'THE DEATH OF CUCHULAIN'* for his mock English Literature O Level. For the benefit of those readers not familiar with Irish Legend, Cuchulain (also spelt Cú Chulainn, Cú Chulaind or Cúchulainn) was a hero of the so called Ulster Cycle and a great and famous warrior.

The Interview: Part I

Spike: Before we begin our conversation, can I just ask you, simply as a matter of interest, why you sent me your essay?

Oliver: Erm ... good question. No, when I saw your advert in the paper I was intrigued more than anything else; I remembered the essay and thought I'd write to you.

Spike: I'm glad you did.

Oliver: How come you accepted it, though? Why include my essay in your book and not somebody else's?

Spike: It's an extremely interesting and amusing essay for one thing.

Oliver: And for another?

Spike: For another, it was the first I received after placing the advertisement.

Oliver: There was a strong element of relief apparent in the extremely fawning letter you wrote back to me.

Spike: And now you know why.

Oliver: Yes ... but I don't entirely understand: what's this book you're writing, perhaps I should say compiling, all about?

Spike: It's about pieces of bizarre and unusual school work.

Oliver: Fascinating.

Spike: I'm glad you think so.

Oliver: But whatever gave you such an 'unusual' idea?

Spike: Erm ... I can't really remember where the idea came from; it's just something I've always wanted to do.

Oliver: Like climbing Mount Everest ... or going to the moon?

Spike: Something like that ... anyway, we'd better get started.

Oliver: Sure.

Spike: You don't mind the tape recorder?

Oliver: No ... I'd have been disappointed if you hadn't brought one along.

Spike: I'm glad I brought it then.

Oliver: It's the mark of a good journalist.

Spike: Thank you.

Oliver: Sorry, I'm putting you off. You were saying?

Spike: Yes ... I'd like to begin by asking you, very briefly, about the context in which you wrote the essay.

Oliver: I wrote it while I was in the fifth form, at High School, in answer to a mock O Level question.

Spike: I should just note for the tape recorder that what was called "fifth form" is nowadays called "year eleven" ... anyway, so you actually wrote the essay under exam conditions, then?

Oliver: That's right: I wrote it in one of the mocks.

Spike: Did you pass the exam?

Oliver: Erm ...

Spike: Sorry, perhaps I shouldn't have asked that.

Oliver: It's all right, I'm not sensitive about failing mocks.

Spike: Then you did fail?

Oliver: What do you think?

Spike: Well, erm ...

Oliver: If you must know, I got about twenty percent.

Spike: About?

Oliver: All right: I got seventeen percent.

Spike: Seventeen percent?

Oliver: Please! Keep your voice down! No, it was just one of those things; I wasn't really bothered at the time.

Spike: Were you bothered later on?

Oliver: Erm ... no, I don't think I was.

Spike: And now?

Oliver: I'm rather proud of getting seventeen percent.

Spike: Did you ever take the final O Level exam?

Oliver: Actually, I did.

Spike: With what result?

Oliver: I passed with grade C.

Spike: I take it there were no questions on 'The Death of Cuchulain'?

Oliver: Ha-ha, you take it correctly; and if there were, I certainly didn't attempt them.

Spike: But you must have written something fairly decent to pass?

Oliver: I did.

Spike: Then your apparent aversion to Yeats didn't apply to other poets?

Oliver: I don't think I was particularly averse to Yeats; I was just indifferent.

Spike: But isn't indifference a type of aversion?

Oliver: Possibly.

Spike: On the work of which poet did you write then?

Oliver: Chesterton.

Spike: G.K.?

Oliver: Naturally.

Spike: And which poem?

Oliver: Lepanto.

Spike: Ah, Lepanto!

Oliver: Quite.

Spike: And were you, in the words of your mock O Level marker, 'able to quote from memory'?

Oliver: I was, yes.

Spike: For example?

Oliver: You want me to quote from memory now?

Spike: If you wouldn't mind.

Oliver: It's been a hell of a long time.

Spike: Nevertheless.

Oliver: All right, I'll have a go ... 'White fonts falling in the courts of the sun, and the Soldan of Byzantium is smiling as they run. There is laughter like the fountains in that face of all men feared, that stirs the forest darkness, the darkness of his beard. It curls the blood red crescent, the crescent of his lips, for the inmost sea of all the world is shaken with his ships. They have dared the white republics up the capes of Italy. They have dashed the Adriatic round the Lion of the sea. And the Pope has cast his arms abroad for agony and loss and called the knights of Christendom for swords about the cross. The cold Queen of England is looking in the glass; the shadow of the Valois is yawning at the mass ...'

Spike: All right! All right! I get the point. I'm very impressed: obviously you quite admired the poem?

Oliver: I admired the first part, yes. Later on, it seemed to fizzle out.

Spike: Fizzle out?

Oliver: Yes, I thought the language deteriorated in a way ... of course, that's only my opinion.

Spike: Of course. Were there any other poets you admired at that time?

Oliver: Erm ... no, I don't think so; at least not amongst the ones I was compelled to study for O Level.

Spike: Do you remember which other poets were on the syllabus?

Oliver: Yes, erm ... there was Burns, Tennyson, Gray and I think Wordsworth.

Spike: And you didn't much care for any of them?

Oliver: Not at the time, no.

Spike: And now?

Oliver: I quite like Wordsworth ... and some Gray.

Spike: What of Burns and Tennyson?

Oliver: No, not really.

Spike: Any particular reason?

Oliver: No, I don't think so. Why is one man's favourite colour blue and another's red?

Spike: A psychologist could probably find answers to both questions.

Oliver: I'm sure he could, though I doubt they'd be the correct ones.

Spike: You could have a point. I'd like to pause for a moment now, while we both read over the essay again. It's at this point in my book that I intend to print your essay - just as you wrote it and without any corrections - preceded by the exam question and followed by the examiner's comment. The reader will then have some idea of what it is we're talking about in the second part of the interview.

Oliver: Fine; should I look at the original?

Spike: Sure, I have a photocopy.

Examination Question

With reference to the text, comment upon the extraordinary economy of language employed by Yeats in his poem, 'The Death of Cuchulain'.

The Essay

Firstly it was by most accounts a good story. The names of the characters were taken from Irish legend. It starts off with Aleel the swineherd reporting to back to Emer in her dun, dun being a very basic type of palace. The story towards the end gets a bit vague. This however does not affect it too much as long as there is somebody who knows about the poem there to explain. Yates (**Yeats!**) does not use a lot of obscure vocabulary, as does Burns in Tam O'Shanter, which clouds over the understanding of the poem. It is by most accounts easy to follow the storyline partly because of this. The story length could, I feel, have been doubled perhaps tripled with some waffle. I think a bit of waffle might not have gone a miss because I think that it is a bit thin in places. Overall, however, Yates (**Yeats!**) dispenses with unnecessary words giving a skeleton poem with a skeleton story. This fulfils the quality of being expressed in an extraordinary economy of language. This is certainly most apt. The Irish civilisation described in this poem is bleak and vague and can be described as a 'skeleton' society. The poem has exactly the same attributes as the thing which it describes. As you read the poem it really gives you a feel of a bleak society. The story fits in with this type of 'no fancy business' poetry as at the end when Cuchulain kills his son it is very abrupt. There's no, 'Oh! Dad how could you do this?' type syndromes - No, Cuchulain kills his son in the most callous manner. It is only after that he mourns him and then with lack of feeling. I think it is a very anti-romantic poem, Emer's dun is no Camelot and Cuchulain is no King Arthur. To say that it deals with human passions is certainly true. It deals with the most basic animal human instincts. The whole plot of the story is centred around this. Cuchulain has gone off with another woman and Emer's going to have him killed for it. This is spite in its most extreme form - Revenge. Also seen in the poem is the characteristic that builds empires - Obedience. Emer tells her son to go and kill a man with the vow has his, to tell no-one his name unless they first beat him in combat. He then goes off to kill a man, why he doesn't care. His mother has told him this man should be killed so off he trots to kill him.

Mark Awarded and Examiner's Remarks

4/20   A 'chatty' vague answer will not do. You cannot avoid the fact that you have no knowledge of the text. To be able to comment on 'the extraordinary economy of language' you must be able to quote from memory. I suggest you get down to some honest work on the texts before it is too late.

The Interview: Part II

Spike: Well ... it's an extraordinary essay.

Oliver: Thanks.

Spike: The examiner's comment is also quite amusing.

Oliver: One of the reasons I sent you the essay: from your advertisement, I thought it was just the kind of thing you wanted.

Spike: It is. In fact, it's almost paradigmatic.

Oliver: You're too kind.

Spike: I did say 'almost'.

Oliver: Of course.

Spike: As a matter of contextual information now, can I just ask you: was the examiner in question your course teacher?

Oliver: Yes.

Spike: He couldn't have been too happy with your exam performance, then?

Oliver: No, I wouldn't have thought so.

Spike: Do you think teachers take this kind of a thing as a personal insult? As an adverse reflection on their teaching methods, I mean?

Oliver: I suppose they must do, to some extent; though that's hardly the problem of their students.

Spike: Of course not. Turning now to the actual content of your teacher's comment, he seems to have been under the impression that you had 'no knowledge of the text'. Do you think his observation was a fair assessment of the situation?

Oliver: Erm ... yes, I think so. Under the circumstances it was probably a very fair comment to make. I did have a rather nebulous recollection of the story-line; but obviously that wasn't enough.

Spike: He writes that 'you cannot avoid the fact that you have no knowledge of the text'; is that or ... was that the case, do you think?

Oliver: I would have avoided 'the fact' a great deal more successfully, if I hadn't spelled the poet's name wrong twice.

Spike: Yes, I noticed that. Quite an unforgivable error really.

Oliver: It is in view of the fact that the correct spelling was given in the question.

Spike: It's the type of slip, if 'slip' is the right word here, that an examiner is not likely to overlook when awarding a mark. I notice that both errors are marked with red ink.

Oliver: I recall somebody commenting at the time that, as far as mistakes are concerned, this falls into the 'dead giveaway' category.

Spike: A nice turn of phrase. Just backtracking a bit now, what about the first sentence of the examiner's comment: 'a "chatty", vague answer will not do' - how do you react to that?

Oliver: You can't really disagree with his observations; beyond doubt, the essay is extremely vague and 'chatty'. Even so, I should say in my defence here, that the name of the game is getting something down onto the answer paper ...

Spike: You're saying that writing a 'chatty' answer is better than writing nothing at all?

Oliver: Absolutely; I got four marks for it ...

Spike: Whereas if you'd written nothing, you wouldn't have got any marks?

Oliver: Precisely; and I ought to point out also, that I did remember the names of three of the characters.

Spike: Impressive.

Oliver: I'm glad you think so.

Spike: Moving on now, let's take a closer look at what you actually wrote.

Oliver: Sure.

Spike: Quite early on in the essay, you observe, and I quote, 'the story towards the end gets a bit vague'.

Oliver: Retrospectively, I feel I might have been tempting fate a little in saying this ...

Spike: Especially if one considers the vagueness of the context in which you say it?

Oliver: Exactly.

Spike: A few lines further on, you suggest, and again I quote, that 'a bit of waffle might not have gone a miss'.

Oliver: That's right.

Spike: What were you trying to do here, exactly?

Oliver: How do you mean?

Spike: Well, it has to be said, that this type of proposition, even if the glaring error at the end is overlooked, should on no account be included in an English Literature examination essay. A suggestion such as this is surely nothing more than a clear indication of desperation; when anything, no matter how ridiculous, will do to fill the page.

Oliver: As I said before, that's the name of the game: no matter how, fill that page!

Spike: Yes ... moving on again, then: while I was reading through the essay for the second time, I noticed that you'd used the word skeleton three times. You mention a 'skeleton poem', a 'skeleton story' and a 'skeleton society'. In a sense what you wrote could fairly be termed - a 'skeleton essay' ...

Oliver: In what way?

Spike: Well ... there's no detail. In fact, the whole essay is little more than an outline, in a sense - a skeleton. So, I ask you, on the basis of my observation: what is the significance of the skeleton metaphor?

Oliver: I really don't think there is one; at least if there is, then I'm not consciously aware of it.

Spike: What about your description of Yeats' work as 'no fancy business poetry'?

Oliver: What about it?

Spike: Couldn't you have thought of anything less ... erm, how shall I say, less obviously silly to write?

Oliver: I probably could have done, given more time, but exams do have time limits.

Spike: Yes, I suppose that's a valid point.

Oliver: I think you have to write what springs to mind.

Spike: But surely you have to apply some form of conscious selection: you can't just write anything!

Oliver: No, there's some truth in that; but it's difficult to draw the dividing line.

Spike: Towards the end of the essay, though, you use the expression: 'with the vow has his'. It seems like complete nonsense; what exactly does it mean?

Oliver: I can't really say. I wondered myself actually, when I was reading through it again, just a moment ago.

Spike: We'll leave that then and move on to the last sentence; and I have to say, to my mind at least, it's this sentence that takes the well fingered, proverbial biscuit. You wrote: 'so off he trots to kill him'.

Oliver: That's right.

Spike: May I ask why?

Oliver: I don't actually remember why, or what I was thinking at the time ...

Spike: To me, the phrase seems indicative of complete apathy on your part.

Oliver: I can't really say.

Spike: This sentence is the last nail in the coffin lid, if you like. It's clearly facetious and therefore by writing it, you must surely have sealed your fate and said goodbye to whatever small chance you had of obtaining a respectable grade.

Oliver: You'd be right, but for one thing: I never, at any point, had any chance of obtaining a respectable grade.

Spike: A fair point.

Oliver: If you're going to fail, you might just as well fail with a smile on your face.

Spike: Mmm ... I've no answer to that. I suppose it's as valid a philosophy as any other.

Oliver: I think so.

Spike: Fair enough. And that, I'm afraid, brings us to the end of your essay.

Oliver: Indeed.

Spike: Thank you very much for speaking to me.

Oliver: My pleasure.

CHAPTER 2: FRENCH LETTERS

Introduction

A few days after I placed an advertisement in a local newspaper asking for someone to send me a copy of any foreign language homework assignment they had done and received a poor mark for, I received a reply from Harry (not his real name – see below) who had written two *creative* pieces as part of his French O Level/GCSE course.

The Interview: Part I

Harry: What's that?

Spike: This?

Harry: Yes: that tie-pin sort of thing?

Spike: It's a microphone.

Harry: You're going to tape our conversation?

Spike: Erm ... yes, if you don't mind. It would interrupt the flow of things if I had to write everything down.

Harry: What if I say something I regret?

Spike: I only want to talk about your French homework: what could you possibly say?

Harry: I don't know: it was a purely hypothetical question.

Spike: OK, after I've typed the interview, I'll send you a copy; if there's anything in it you think might be embarrassing, I'll get rid of it.

Harry: Are you sure you can get rid of things so easily?

Spike: How do you mean?

Harry: Some things aren't as easy to get rid of as others.

Spike: I'm not with you?

Harry: It's elementary: the printed word derives power from its author - it can be difficult to overcome that power later on.

Spike: Sure ... but in this case I don't think there'll be any problem.

Harry: Are you certain of that?

Spike: I'm absolutely positive.

Harry: That's all right then; but you promise to send me a copy of the interview before it's published?

Spike: I absolutely assure you.

Harry: Fair enough.

Spike: If we can begin then...

Harry: What about my name?

Spike: Your name?

Harry: Yes, you understand that I want to remain completely anonymous?

Spike: Absolutely. I refer to my interviewees only by their first name - I can even use another first name if you like.

Harry: I'd be a lot happier if you'd do that for me.

Spike: Certainly ... now, if there isn't...

Harry: No, there's nothing else, you can begin whenever you're ready.

Spike: Thanks. Before we talk about the letters, I'd just like to build up some background information, if ...

Harry: What kind of background information?

Spike: How long did you study French, for example?

Harry: Oh ... well, I had my first French lesson when I was eleven years old, the day after I started at Secondary school, as I remember.

Spike: How long did you study French?

Harry: Five and a half years in total.

Spike: And during what stage of those five and a half years did you produce these pieces of erm ... of work.

Harry: Why did you pause then?

Spike: When?

Harry: Just then, when you said, 'these pieces'; you paused before you said 'work'.

Spike: I didn't intend to.

Harry: But you paused!

Spike: I'm sorry.

Harry: Why did you do it then?

Spike: There was no reason ...

Harry: There was! There was! You were going to say pieces of crap, weren't you?

Spike: No, whatever gave you that impression?

Harry: I know what you're thinking. I know why you paused. Deny it if you like, but I know why you paused. I don't have to submit myself to this kind of ridicule you know!

Spike: Look, I'm not trying to ridicule you, all right?

Harry: No, it isn't all right! I don't have to stand for this!

Spike: You answered my advert in the paper; nobody made you come here.

Harry: There's no need to be like that, is there? I'm perfectly willing to discuss my work with you.

Spike: Good ... perhaps we could continue, then?

Harry: Certainly.

Spike: Could you begin by answering my question then; at what stage...

Harry: Yes, yes; I know what the question was! As you can see from the dates on the top of the pages; I produced the first piece of work on the 15th of September and the second a couple of weeks later. It was the Autumn Term of 1983. I was in the Fifth Form and due to take my mock O Levels that Christmas.

Spike: I see, so these two pieces of work represent at least four full years of French?

Harry: Yes, in a way ... no! I really don't see how you can say 'four full years of French'; you can't possibly say 'four full years of French'; I mean, how the hell can you possibly say that?

Spike: What do you mean?

Harry: 'Full'! 'Full'! Those years weren't 'full' of French: they were virtually devoid of it!

Spike: You blame the method of teaching for your failure then?

Harry: 'Failure'? What do you mean 'Failure'? It wasn't my failure; it was theirs!

Spike: Who are they?

Harry: All of them! The teachers, the examiners, the people who wrote the textbooks, the people who designed the course, the government ... yes, especially the government: it was a Conservative government at the time.

Spike: It is now.

Harry: Exactly, but I'm not studying French any more. I shouldn't need to; but Jacques Delors, he was doing a good job.

Spike: I'm sorry?

Harry: For what?

Spike: You mentioned Jacques Delors?

Harry: That's right: he was doing a good job.

Spike: Fine ... I know what you mean; but getting back to the question of your ... I mean, the circumstances leading up to your erm ... getting back, I mean, to the events leading up to the examiners' unwillingness to grant you a pass grade in French 'O'-Level: do you feel now that those years of French were wasted?

Harry: Wasted! Completely wasted! I was failed by the system. You know what they say about the best way to learn French ...

Spike: There's no doubt some truth in it, but leaving that discussion aside for the moment, if I may, I'd like really to turn now to the two pieces of work you sent to me. They both take the form of letters; is there any reason for that?

Harry: Of course, there is! We were following a structured course. We had a text book; the question probably said something like: 'write a letter to your such and such, about so and so', or something like that.

Spike: So, you were told to write letters.

Harry: I was told to, yes, we all were: we were only following orders.

Spike: Orders?

Harry: I really don't know what else you could call them; try to disobey if you like - you know the consequences.

Spike: Right, I know what you're saying but let's move to the first piece of work now.

Harry: Whatever you like, you know best - you seem to think you do anyway.

Spike: Sure.

Unfortunately lost, but something along the lines of: "Imagine you are a young man called Yves, who has just moved from Amiens to Paris. Write to your mother about your new life in Paris."

Original (uncorrected) French Text

Septembre 15.

Chere maman,

Je suis arrive a Paris ce matin, le samedi. Il est vingt-trois heures maintenant je vient de finir mon travail pour auijourd'hui. L'idee me a venu que je dois ecrire a ma cher maman. Ma vie ici, en paris, est tres different que il serait en Amiens. Quand je suis sorti la gare ce matin, huit heures, il y avait beaucoup de commotion au centre de ville. J'ai demande un agent que se passerait. L'agent a dit moi que un avion de bombardement francais, qui volait a travers la manche, accrocherait la foch a sept heures et demie et aussi le president aux etuds sortait sa maison a six heures quattre. Quand j'ai dit, 'et', l'agent a commence parler, 'Le president, monsieur Reagan, portait rouge pantalons et non veste. Aussi il portait impairs chausettes avec non chaussures. Maintenant Je dois aller pour regarder le neuf desastre. Un etandard avion de combat a accroche la Tour Eiffel et tuerais douze personnes il-y-a 40 minutes.

Au revoir, Yves.

September 15th.

Dear Mum,

I arrived in Paris this morning, Saturday. It is twenty-three hours now I have just finished my work for today. The idea just came to me that I should write to my dear mum. My life here, in Paris, is very different to what it was in Amiens. When I left the station, eight hours, there was a lot of commotion in the centre of town. I asked a policeman what was going on. The policeman told me that a French fighter plane, that wanted to go across the channel, had crashed into the Foch at seven hours and a half and also the president of the states was leaving his house at six hours four. When I said, 'and', the policeman began to talk, 'The president, Mr. Reagan, was wearing red trousers and no shirt. Also, he was wearing odd socks with no shoes. Now I must go to look at the new disaster. A fighter plane crashed into the Eiffel Tower and killed twelve people 40 minutes ago.

Good-bye, Yves.

Mark and Teacher's Comment

10/20   Please don't let your wild imagination prevent you from writing correct French. I did not want an imaginative piece - I wanted a re-hash of classwork to show you understood the different tense uses. You do not have sufficient command of the language yet to write such complicated stories. I'm afraid you must concentrate on correct grammar to pass O Level. Imagination is not required in a French O Level essay - (Unfortunately)

The Interview: Part II

Spike: I'd like to talk first, very briefly, about the language before turning to the actual content.

Harry: Fine. Fine. That's absolutely fine.

Spike: As you can see, I have here the actual page, torn from your exercise book, containing the letter in question. The first thing I notice is the profusion of red circles and crosses. Does the actual amount of red ink on the page give a good indication of the standard of the French you used in the letter?

Harry: What a load of crap!

Spike: I'm sorry?

Harry: I hope you didn't drag me half way across the city to ask poxy questions like that! Of course, the red ink gives an indication of the standard of French. If the French had been correct the teacher wouldn't have bloody well corrected it, would she?

Spike: No, that's true ...

Harry: Well, why ask such patently rhetorical questions then? Haven't you got anything better to do with your time?

Spike: Moving on to the mark you received now; do you think it was fair?

Harry: How should I know? I don't speak French!

Spike: I can see that from your letters.

Harry: Look, have you got anything sensible to say or are you just trying to make me look like a pleb?

Spike: Why did you write that your 'life in Paris is very different to what it was in Amiens'?

Harry: Because it was different.

Spike: But you didn't live in Paris when you wrote it.

Harry: I was trying to place myself in the position of the fictional Yves.

Spike: Ah, yes ... I see; and do we take it then, that this fictional Yves had moved from Amiens to Paris.

Harry: You do.

Spike: Why Amiens? Why not St. Tropez or Nice?

Harry: Why St. Tropez or Nice? Why not Lyons or Toulouse?

Spike: You're saying, in a rather roundabout way, that Amiens was chosen at random?

Harry: No, I'm not; I'm saying, in a rather roundabout way, that it was a damned silly question - like all the others. What you should have asked was: 'Was there any particular reason that Yves came from Amiens?'

Spike: Well? Was there?

Harry: Yes, as a matter of fact there was. The study of modern languages, as you are no doubt already aware, often involves the pursuit of some incredibly trite and nauseating fictional, foreign family.

Spike: Are you trying to say that this fictional Yves was a member of some such fictional, foreign family?

Harry: No, I'm not trying to say it - I am saying it, you see the nuance?

Spike: Yes.

Harry: And to prevent any further meanderings on the point, I'll add for the sake of all concerned that I, and those you studied alongside me, were told...

Spike: Wouldn't 'requested' be a far more pleasant phrase.

Harry: Yes, that's very clever; I've seen Casablanca as well, now shut up and let me get on with what I'm saying.

Spike: Sure.

Harry: We were told to write a letter from the fictional Yves to his no less fictional mother, concerning his departure from Amiens to take up residence in Paris. We were told that we were to highlight the differences in lifestyle that he experienced as a result of his relocation.

Spike: But your letter doesn't do that, does it?

Harry: No, why should it? It's a thoroughly boring exercise.

Spike: If I may say so though, you made a mistake in your logic didn't you?

Harry: What do you mean?

Spike: You do in fact say quite plainly in the letter, and I quote: 'My life here, in Paris, is very different to what it was in Amiens'.

Harry: All right, so I made some attempt to answer the question, what of it? I hardly think that constitutes a logical error.

Spike: But you also say earlier on, speaking in the person of the fictional Yves, that you arrived in Paris 'this morning', on the morning in fact that you wrote the words 'My life here, in Paris, is very different to what it was in Amiens'. Now my question is simply this: how can you make such a generalized statement about the difference in lifestyles when you have been in Paris for less than a day and by clear implication, not even spent a night there? Is that not, in fact, a clear error in reasoning?

Harry: No, it isn't. Let me ask you this: how long would I have to live in Paris to be able to make the statement reasonably?

Spike: More than a day.

Harry: A day and a half?

Spike: No ... longer than that.

Harry: How long then? Three days? Seven days? Thirty years?

Spike: About a week then.

Harry: Would six days do?

Spike: No.

Harry: Why not?

Spike: Because I said a week.

Harry: There are exactly 168 hours in a week.

Spike: So, what?

Harry: Would 167 hours be long enough?

Spike: No.

Harry: Why not?

Spike: Because I want to be as pedantic as you.

Harry: You're wrong then, aren't you?

Spike: No, I'm not: you're the one who's wrong, I think.

Harry: No, you're wrong; but that seems to be a way of life for you.

Spike: All right. Perhaps we should move on to the main point of your letter now.

Harry: All right.

Spike: What's this business about a French fighter plane crashing into the Foch?

Harry: It's nothing; the sentence is in French and that's about it.

Spike: What is the Foch?

Harry: A French aircraft carrier.

Spike: Why was Mr. Reagan dressed so oddly?

Harry: No reason at all.

Spike: Is the last sentence a springboard for the second letter?

Harry: That's the first sensible question you've asked me! I'm pleased to say that it isn't, at least, not in that sense. Although you're absolutely right that the second letter does follow directly from this one and starts where this one finishes, with the point about the Eiffel Tower. But the priorities have to be reversed, I think. The second letter might spring from this one, but the last sentence isn't intentionally a springboard for the second letter ... no - I really don't think so.

Spike: What about the teacher's comment, at the end of the letter.

Harry: Thanks, I know where to find it ... I don't agree with it at all - it's a nonsense.

Spike: It seems quite reasonable to me. Why do you call it a nonsense?

Harry: The teacher states that she 'did not want an imaginative piece' but that is clearly untrue; she did want an imaginative piece.

Spike: Why do you say that?

Harry: Elementary, my dear Spike. I was asked to write a letter detailing the difference in lifestyle between Paris and Amiens. I was asked also to place myself in the position of this so-called Yves. Now, it has to be said, that I have never been either to Paris or Amiens - also my name is not Yves - how then can I possibly write about the difference between Paris and Amiens other than by imagining what that difference might be? I would suggest that my teacher took exception not to my using my imagination but to what I imagined with it. Thus, her final statement is wholly incorrect because imagination is required in a French O Level essay, unless the essay question deals specifically with the experience of the candidate, which this one - it must be admitted - does not.

Spike: That's a very fair point, I have to admit. Let's move on now to the second letter you sent me.

Harry: As you wish.

Homework Question

Also, unfortunately lost, but something along the lines of: "Write to your friend about your day trip to Paris."

Original (uncorrected) French Text

Septembre 34, 1983.

Ma chere amie,

hier je suis alle a Paris. Cet etait un bon jour et maintenant je suis tres riche. Je vais dire une grande confession qui concerne mon hier activites. Tu sais que la Tour Eiffel, hier matin, avait un accident. Un etandard de combat a attroche La Tour Eiffel et l'a detruisis. Mais je te dit que cet n'est pas vrai. Hier JE, oui, JE avec mon grand pigeon ont donne la tour l'accident. Ou est la tour ma amie? Ou sont les restes? Oui! Ou sont-ils? Tu ne sais pas! n'est pas? Mon pigeon a mange la tour pour son petit dejeurner et il te mangera si tu dit a la police ma confession.

Au revoir.

P.S. Il-y-a une canne courbe ici?

September 34th, 1983.

My dear friend (female),

yesterday I went to Paris. It was a good day and now I am very rich. I am going to make a great confession which concerns my activities of yesterday. You know that the Eiffel Tower, yesterday morning, met with an accident. A combat aircraft crashed into the Eiffel Tower and destroyed it. But I tell you that it is not true. Yesterday I, yes, I with my giant pigeon caused the accident to the tower. Where is the tower now, my friend? Where are the pieces? Yes! Where are they? You don't know! Do you? My pigeon ate the tower for his breakfast and he will eat you if you tell the police my confession.

Good-bye.

P.S. Is there a bent stick here?

Teacher's Comment

DO YOU WANT TO PASS O LEVEL OR NOT?

HAVE YOU READ MY LAST NOTE?

I WILL NOT READ ANY MORE OF YOUR FANTASIES!!

The Interview: Part III

Spike: Let me start by asking you about the circumstances in which you devised this letter: did this piece of work immediately proceed the last letter, or did you produce other more orthodox pieces of work in between?

Harry: As I remember it, this was the next piece of 'creative' work I undertook in French. Of course, the letters were punctuated timewise by more mundane exercises such as comprehensions and the like; but those things simply don't provide the scope to be humorous.

Spike: Why did you date the letter 'September 34th, 1983'?

Harry: Because I wrote it on the fourth of October.

Spike: Erm ... oh, yes. But erm...

Harry: Look! It's perfectly obvious: isn't it?

Spike: Yes, I suppose it is. Moving on then, I notice that your teacher never bothered to correct the French this time, she just put a red line through the whole thing and wrote her comment underneath. Why was that do you think?

Harry: You mean, why didn't she correct the French?

Spike: Yes.

Harry: I can only speculate naturally.

Spike: Naturally.

Harry: I suppose she was angry that I'd ignored her last comment.

Spike: That was quite a reasonable reaction, don't you think?

Harry: No, I don't. The purpose in writing these silly letters is supposedly to practise one's French, to practise the construction of sentences et cetera. Now, to my mind it doesn't matter whether a person writes that a giant pigeon ate the Eiffel Tower or that a friend of theirs went to a party and ate too much cheese. One can only assume that if I'd written the latter I would have escaped censure.

Spike: Turning back for just a moment to the teacher's comment on the first letter you wrote, I'd like to draw your attention to the point that was made about your not having 'sufficient command of the language yet to write such complicated stories'.

Harry: I accept that the first of the letters contained some rather complicated structures which, admittedly, I didn't have sufficient understanding of to use correctly; but as regards the second letter I don't think that this was the case at all; no, I simply don't accept that.

Spike: But surely a story about a giant pigeon eating the Eiffel Tower is complicated, isn't it?

Harry: No, not at all, I simply don't accept that. In what sense is it complicated? The plot is hardly intricate, the grammatical structures needed to express it are fairly rudimentary. No, I don't accept that it's complicated; it's simply not orthodox.

Spike: Do you think then, that the lack of orthodoxy was the offending aspect of your work?

Harry: I would say so yes. You see, my point is: if instead, I'd written that I won a fortune in a casino and then gone pigeon racing with couple of friends, would that have drawn the same reaction?

Spike: There's no way of knowing, is there?

Harry: Not for certain, I'll admit, but I'd guess not.

Spike: Yes, you're probably right; but let me ask you then, why didn't you write that you'd won a fortune in a casino and then gone pigeon racing?

Harry: The story I wrote was less complicated, from a structural - though possibly not from a conceptual - point of view. If you look at it closely, you'll see that it required very little vocabulary.

Spike: Are you saying then, that this kind of story is easier to write than a more orthodox one?

Harry: I'm surprised you even bother to ask: it's absolutely obvious. The logic is simple; if you write the usual crap - I got up at such and such a time, I caught the bus, I went to the Louvre, I had lunch on the left bank - all the examiner does is look at the French; if you write something like this, the examiner could just possibly fail to notice a mistake while he read ahead, skipping over the words in his subconscious pursuit of the story.

Spike: Are you defending what you wrote on the basis that something out of the ordinary could get you more marks?

Harry: Shall we say less marks knocked off for spelling and grammatical errors.

Spike: That's rather a subversive approach to O Level French, isn't it?

Harry: When fortune compels one to sit an examination in a subject one knows precious little about, one has to resort to unusual methods. Pragmatism is always the best approach; and as they say, necessity is the mother of invention.

Spike: On the basis of what you've said, I feel compelled to ask: why did you take French at all?

Harry: When I selected my O Level options in the third year, I was led to believe that I would need a modern language to gain entrance into a university.

Spike: Did that turn out to be false then?

Harry: It did indeed, at the end of the fourth year I learnt that Latin would be acceptable for matriculation purposes.

Spike: So, you'd taken French for nothing then?

Harry: Exactly.

Spike: Just as a matter of interest, how did you do in the actual French O Level exam?

Harry: I failed.

Spike: And in Latin?

Harry: I got an A.

Spike: I suppose that really answers my first question about the teacher's comment: 'Do you want to pass O level or not'.

Harry: I suppose it does, yes.

Spike: Turning to what you wrote in the letter now, I have to say that on re-examining it, it is a fairly simple story - unusual but simple. The one thing about the letter which really does puzzle me is the post script: 'Is there a bent stick here?'

Harry: I can tell you about that, if you like.

Spike: Please, I'd like very much.

Harry: Very well: it's a reference to the thirteenth century Cathar heresy of Languedoc.

Spike: Languedoc, Southern France?

Harry: Precisely; you see the connection now?

Spike: Other than that Languedoc is in Southern France, and its inhabitants presumably speak French, I can't see any connection at all, no. Leaving that completely aside for the moment though, what exactly is the phrase 'is there a bent stick here' supposed to mean?

Harry: It was a kind of code used by the Cathars when they entered a strange house.

Spike: They'd ask if there was a bent stick in the house?

Harry: Precisely.

Spike: And what exactly would constitute 'a bent stick'?

Harry: A Catholic, especially a priest or member of one of the orders. They could alternatively say: Greetings may we better ourselves here.

Spike: I see.

Harry: No, I don't think you do see: this is an extremely salient point.

Spike: In what way?

Harry: By placing it at the beginning of the letter it might have dissuaded the uninitiated from reading it.

Spike: Are you saying that you might have received a better hearing had this letter been marked by a Cathar?

Harry: It's possible, yes.

Spike: Though most unlikely, I think.

Harry: Think what you like.

Spike: I'd like to move on now to the statement your teacher concluded her comment with: 'I will not read any more of your fantasies!' This ties in very nicely, also, with the question of why you wrote what you did, in particular why you chose to write about a giant pigeon. Is the pigeon some sort of metaphor for world communism or something?

Harry: There is without doubt a metaphor in operation here, and I do recall it having something vaguely to do with communism - you'll no doubt recall the sentence from the first letter in which I described the president of the United States wearing red trousers.

Spike: So, the trousers were a communism metaphor then?

Harry: Undoubtedly, but as to the pigeon metaphor ... well, I could do no more than speculate at this point.

Spike: A pity. Moving on to something else then; your teacher used the word 'fantasies' in her comment. Did you then, or do you now, fantasize about giant pigeons?

Harry: Never ... only spider monkeys.

Spike: I'm sorry?

Harry: I said: spider monkeys, or to be more precise, spider monkey.

Spike: So, you have fantasies about a spider monkey?

Harry: No, I only have one fantasy and even then, only while listening to Rossini.

Spike: Why did you choose a giant pigeon as your ally then, why not a giant spider monkey?

Harry: The spider monkey fantasy is really quite recent, far more recent than the letter anyway.

Spike: Do you think the spider monkey fantasy evolved in some way from the giant pigeon fantasy?

Harry: Look, I've already told you that I've never fantasised about pigeons - giant, metaphors for world communism, or otherwise.

Spike: OK.

Harry: You're damned right it's OK!

Spike: I hope you won't think me too forward for asking this, but I really can't help myself. What exactly is the form of this spider monkey fantasy; and how does it fit in with Rossini?

Harry: Very briefly then: about three months ago I became aware of the fact that every time I listened to any of Rossini's overtures, especially *L'italiana in Algeri*, *La gazza ladra* and *La scala di seta*, I could see a spider monkey jumping up and down on the postcard stands in Llandudno's Mostyn Street. It was as if it - the spider monkey I mean - was making progress through the shoppers, swinging on the awnings and postcard stands ... all the time to the tune of Rossini's overtures.

Spike: How amazing!

Harry: Closing my eyes I can see it now: deee, de, de, dee, dee, dee, dum, de, dee, de, de, de, dee, dum, de, deee, deee, de ...

Spike: What are you doing?

Harry: Rossini!! I can't fight it anymore! I can see the spider monkey!

Spike: What's it doing?

Harry: Swinging, always swinging ... I can't fight it anymore! I just walk along beside it.

Spike: In your fantasy this is?

Harry: Exactly.

Spike: Do you experience the same vision every time?

Harry: It always starts in the same place: Mostyn Street. It all depends on how much Rossini I listen to, though. The more overtures I play, the longer the fantasy becomes. Only yesterday the spider monkey went all the way down to the West Shore and began to jump on children's sandcastles ... I really don't know where it will end.

Spike: Astonishing! Absolutely astonishing!

Harry: It is! It is!

Spike: Thank you for sharing that with us. It really is one of the most astounding things I've ever heard. Unfortunately, due to the lateness of the hour, I'm afraid we shall have to leave it there.

Harry: Has it been a successful interview?

Spike: It has indeed, almost certainly the most rewarding I've done so far. I'd hesitate to describe it as an interview, though, there were times when I felt that it was you who was interviewing me.

Harry: A conversation then?

Spike: A conversation indeed; and, shall I say - I consider our conversation to have been extremely beneficial, especially as it progressed, towards the end, far beyond the scope of my original intentions.

Harry: Thank you for agreeing to speak to me.

Spike: I'm supposed to say that!

Harry: Go on then, say it.

Spike: Thank you for agreeing to speak to me.

Harry: Thank you.

CHAPTER 3: REGARDING THE DESIGN OF SHOPPING PRECINCTS

Introduction

A few days after I placed an advertisement in a local newspaper asking for someone to send me a copy of any essay which they had written in preparation for General Studies A Level, I received a reply from Andrew who had written what I considered to be an interesting piece *Regarding the Design of Shopping Precincts* - malls as they're known in the US.

The Interview: Part I

Andrew: ... is there a problem?

Spike: I forgot to turn my tape recorder on ...

Andrew: You have it in your shirt?

Spike: Yes ... see.

Andrew: May I?

Spike: Sure.

Andrew: I've never seen one this small.

Spike: Quite an expensive little item that.

Andrew: I can imagine: must have cost you a few hundred?

Spike: Well, you're close. Anyway, let's get back to what you were saying; I'm afraid I've rather put you off.

Andrew: I was just saying that I can't honestly imagine that there'll be much of a market for a book like the one you're writing about people's school work.

Spike: Only time will tell.

Andrew: I suppose if you don't try you'll never know.

Spike: Well, this is it; a man has to have something to hope for.

Andrew: What about all the hours you put in, though? Won't you feel that all the time and effort will have been wasted if it doesn't do well?

Spike: There's no sacrifice too great for a chance at immortality!

Andrew: Bogart?

Spike: By gad, Sir!

Andrew: Ha-ha-ha ... fancy that: another Bogart fan.

Spike: I'd better stop you there, before we get off onto another side-track. Let's take a look at your essay, shall we? Then we can talk about some of the points you raised in it.

Andrew: Sure.

Assignment Question

Unfortunately, the original question has been lost, but it was something along the lines of: "If a new shopping precinct were to be built in your area, what advice would you give to the architect."

The Essay

If a new shopping precinct was to be built in my approximate locality I may well have some advice to give to the architect. By the experience I have had personally at precincts of various descriptions I feel that many things are wrong with many precincts. The first type of advice I would give to the architect would be safety considerations. The shopping precinct should have wide corridors so that there is no crush, the ceiling should be high to allow the circulation of air, there should be a multitude of fire precautions; and concerning these fellows there is more to be mentioned.

The fires that sometimes start in places of this nature are very often due to planning negligence. The places where electrical cables are to be run should have no flammable materials around them. The buildings should not be erected in such a way as to lead the electricians to put too little care into the installation of such cables. The architect would do well, in my opinion, to consult both the fire department and the electricians so they can all plan together the design of the building's electrical installations. The architect should place a reasonable amount of stone stairwells with no flammable materials in them to allow the public to escape to relative safety in the most unfortunate event of a fire. The lights should all be fitted with breaking devices to stop them smashing into the floor at high velocities in the event of a most unfortunate occurrence. Fire hose ports should be placed well and not in such way that the public can do damage to them. **(RATHER TOO LONG JUST ON ONE THEME)**

I think the architect should talk to the police about many corridors for snipers in the most unfortunate event of an hostage situation. The police could then shoot all the subversives dead without risking the public's wellbeing. The actual design of the shopping floor is of further consideration.

The shops should all be placed so that their fronts are in clear sight of the guards' office so that any yobs (undesirable social elements) exiting the shops with stolen goods could be apprehended. If the shopping area was like a labyrinth such individuals might find the layout to their best advantage in eluding the forces of the law. I think the architect would be well advised to find out what sort of commodities were to be retailed in the volumes he is designing.

Some shops are not suitably designed for the items they sell. The architect should take into consideration the kind of shelves and counters needed,

'I don't know what kind of shops there are going to be,' he might say, to which I might reply,

'Well why don't you find out then because there's not much point in building a shopping centre if nobody is interested in occupying a shop there.' **(POINT IS UNWORTHY OF MAKING SO MUCH OF)**

If the shopping centre is more than forty stories high then it will be too big, I think. **(IS THIS MEANT SERIOUSLY?)**

I feel that in order for the architect to make a good accounting of himself he should make the outside of the building look reasonably decent and not like the Newcastle branch of Fine Fare which is an absolutely splendid example of ugliness and complete lack of colour co-ordination. I think that Fine Fare would look a lot 'nicer' if it had some turrets and flags and looked like a medieval castle. Then it would give the town some real character. I don't like some sorts of modern architecture because it is grotesque.

Grade Awarded and Teacher's Comment.

Grade F

This essay is mostly nonsense. If you intend me to mark your work or teach you - I expect to see a more serious application.

The Interview: Part II

Spike: If we can start by discussing the grade you got for the essay?

Andrew: I got an F.

Spike: That indicates an A Level fail, doesn't it?

Andrew: Yes.

Spike: As a matter of interest, how did you do in the actual 'A'-Level exam?

Andrew: I passed.

Spike: With what grade?

Andrew: Grade A.

Spike: Isn't that rather odd, in light of this essay mark?

Andrew: No, I don't think so. You see, to my mind, the essays I did during the *course*, in inverted commas, were simply an exercise in frivolity; but when I took the exam, I wrote something sensible and coherent.

Spike: Why do you say, 'course, in inverted commas'?

Andrew: General Studies is just that - general. It's a practical impossibility to cover all, to cover even five percent in fact, of the areas of human knowledge that could possibly come up on the actual exam paper.

Spike: Do you think it's a waste of time to have General Studies lessons then?

Andrew: You're asking me, but I would hate to make a general statement on this; what isn't helpful for one person might well be helpful for another.

Spike: Let me rephrase the question then: was it a waste of time for you to attend General Studies lessons?

Andrew: It would have been, if I hadn't used the time to amuse myself.

Spike: What exactly do you mean by 'amuse myself'?

Andrew: It's quite simple: if I'd written the essays that were set properly, and by that I mean coherently and sensibly, then it would have (a) taken a long time to write them and (b) been entirely useless due to the improbability of the same essay question being set on the actual A Level paper. You understand?

Spike: Yes, I see the point you're making. You're saying that there was no examination orientated reason for you to apply yourself to the General Studies lessons or the homework that stemmed from them.

Andrew: That's right.

Spike: Wasn't that a rather elitist stance to adopt though?

Andrew: No, I don't think so; I was simply trying to make life interesting.

Spike: And you made life interesting by writing essays that your teacher described as 'mostly nonsense'?

Andrew: That's one of the tactics I employed to brighten things up a little, yes.

Spike: There were others, then?

Andrew: Naturally, there were several; but do you really want me to go into them now?

Spike: No. It would probably be better not to ... for the time being at least. Let's get back to your essay.

Andrew: All right.

Spike: How did you feel about the grade you received?

Andrew: I think 'F' was the right grade; if I written something similar in the exam I would have expected to fail.

Spike: And what about the comment 'this essay is mostly nonsense'?

Andrew: Again, I don't think that was at all unfair. The reasons for which my teacher thought the essay nonsense are certainly plain enough.

Spike: What are they, do you think?

Andrew: The continual repetition of ludicrous phrases, the making of facetious and irrelevant points, the obvious lack of effort to address the question - to name but a few.

Spike: Let's look more closely at some of those points then and try to find some examples of them in your text.

Andrew: Certainly, why not?

Spike: Why not indeed, and perhaps by following that path we might be able to find some method to your madness and gain some sort of insight into the methods you were using at that time.

Andrew: I don't honestly think that there was a method to what you call 'my madness'. Also, as far as insights are concerned, I can't for the life of me see what possible purpose they could serve if they were to be gained.

Spike: Let me worry about the purpose of things.

Andrew: As you like it.

Spike: Let's begin then: the first point I think worthy of mention is the replacement of the word 'area', from the question, by the phrase 'approximate locality'. This is no doubt a taste of what is to follow: but what possible reason could there have been for such a portending substitution? Were you perhaps, even at so early a stage in the essay, trying to be amusing?

Andrew: No, I don't really think so: after all, the substitution is not all that hilarious, is it?

Spike: No, not really.

Andrew: I feel, retrospectively, that the substitution you pointed out was some sort of primitive attempt at a literary vaccination.

Spike: 'A literary vaccination'? What the devil is that?

Andrew: It is, if you like, an indication of what is to follow in a way. Perhaps a kind of watered down example of the sort of phrases that are going to be used later on.

Spike: Something to prepare the reader for far more chimerical expressions then?

Andrew: That's about it, yes. I think something like that gets the reader slightly used to the fact that some of the phrases that are going to appear may not be erm ... may not be normal.

Spike: What do you mean by 'normal'?

Andrew: Well, the kind of thing one would 'normally' expect to find in a General Studies essay.

Spike: So that's what you mean by the term 'literary vaccination'?

Andrew: Yes, I think so.

Spike: It's a pretty grandiose idea, if you don't mind my saying so.

Andrew: I don't mind at all; although I have to admit that the concept I've outlined may well have been developed after the essay was written.

Spike: You're suggesting that your intention in substituting 'approximate locality' for 'area' might not have been to make a literary vaccination then?

Andrew: It's possible; I don't remember.

Spike: Let's move on then, to another point. I notice from the original of the essay, that your teacher made several marks to indicate where she felt new paragraphs should have started.

Andrew: That's right, I don't think I'd separated things out the way she wanted.

Spike: From the look of things, she would have preferred you to have had a separate paragraph for each different point of advice.

Andrew: Yes.

Spike: Was she right, do you think?

Andrew: Yes, I think so; that would seem the logical thing to have done.

Spike: Why didn't you do that at the time, then? Was it part of your curriculum of amusement or just a structural oversight on your part?

Andrew: I think it was a structural oversight; but having said that, I make no apology for it. This essay was probably written in about ten to fifteen minutes. I never planned essays or gave even the least bit of thought to what I was going to write. My usual practice in the writing of essays was to think as I wrote and to write as I thought; and acting thus, in such an unpremeditated state, to set down my conceptions of reality.

Spike: It's hardly surprising then that there are so many spelling and grammatical errors. But what about the statement you made about having had experience of 'precincts of various descriptions'? Was that true or not?

Andrew: It wasn't particularly true ... or false, for that matter. Suffice it to say, it's truer now than it was then, and would have been less true when I was ten than it was when I wrote the essay.

Spike: It would be fair to say then, that you did have some actual information on shopping precincts in your memory bank.

Andrew: Absolutely.

Spike: Moving on to look at the remainder of the first paragraph now, it's nearly all sensible, for want of a better word. The first real hint of anything less than what could be considered 'a serious application' is seen in the word 'multitude'. Although such a usage could hardly be thought damningly reprehensible it is not altogether appropriate either, is it?

Andrew: Again, I think it's use fits in with the idea of the literary vaccination which we were talking about earlier.

Spike: What about the structure that follows shortly afterwards: 'and concerning these fellows there is more to be mentioned'?

Andrew: That's the first of the explicitly foolish utterances; I think my amusement effectively started there.

Spike: But then it stops, doesn't it?

Andrew: In the second paragraph you mean?

Spike: Yes, what's the reason for that do you think?

Andrew: I'm not so sure it does stop actually: I think it just becomes subtler.

Spike: You mean that it still amused you, even though it wasn't overtly facetious?

Andrew: That's right.

Spike: But the second paragraph does go some way towards, and by that I mean in the direction of, answering the question.

Andrew: That's a fair criticism. Had I had more time to write, I'm sure I could have thought of something inaner to say.

Spike: You did manage to get something in there, though. The point made about stone stairwells is certainly fair enough to begin with, but the use of the expression 'relative safety', where just plain 'safety' would have done, certainly smacks of something distinctly dubious in this context.

Andrew: It's not a particularly noteworthy expression, I have to admit, but I think the purpose of it was to express the contention, which is certainly true, that safety is relative and that nowhere is absolutely safe.

Spike: In a sense, then, it was a philosophical point?

Andrew: If you like, yes.

Spike: What about the end of that sentence, which is, if you like, the *pièce de résistance*?

Andrew: The concluding phrase, you mean - 'in the most unfortunate event of a fire'?

Spike: Yes. 'In the event of a fire' would certainly have sufficed; 'in the unfortunate event of a fire' might arguably have been admissible on the basis that the word 'unfortunate' might be seen to lend a more human and less specifically physical dimension to such an eventuality; but surely the word 'most' was quite uncalled for?

Andrew: My teacher seems to have thought so; as you can see she, put a red line through it.

Spike: What about the astonishing point you made in the fifth sentence: that the lights should be fitted with 'breaking devices'?

Andrew: Yes, but I rather think I ruined that particular suggestion by misspelling 'braking'.

Spike: Yes, I thought when I read it, that it wasn't the right kind of 'braking'.

Andrew: A pity, that.

Spike: What exactly did you intend to mean by 'braking devices' though? At a precursory glance it seems like exceptional drivel.

Andrew: I beg to differ. Allow me to elucidate the point. One often sees 'disaster movies' these days set in large American cities ...

Spike: Indeed, most of which are disasters in themselves.

Andrew: I can't disagree with you on that point. But as I was saying; in these so-called disaster movies, one almost invariably sees grand, ornate chandeliers descending from on high and subsequently smashing into thousands of pieces over the heads of swarming extras. By 'braking devices', I meant parachutes or rubber cords or something of a similar function to prevent this from happening should the chandeliers for some reason become separated from the precinct ceiling.

Spike: What an astonishing idea.

Andrew: I'm glad you think so.

Spike: But no sooner is this ridiculous suggestion about braking devices fielded, than 'most unfortunate' appears again, this time with 'occurrence' tied to its tail.

Andrew: The allusion here is to the flogging of a dead horse for those who missed it.

Spike: I could ask you what exactly you mean by that, but at this juncture in our conversation, I somehow don't think I'll bother. Instead, let's turn directly to your teacher's comment, which appears at about this point.

Andrew: I think the comment's reasonably fair, given the length of the essay.

Spike: You're saying then, that you think the length of the essay is not such as to merit so prolix a section purely on the theme of safety.

Andrew: That's about it, yes.

Spike: Let's move on to the next paragraph then. To my mind, it's here that the gradual decline in seriousness of intent really begins in proper.

A far more daring approach to the essay becomes evident, if you like. From here on the essay changes, it metamorphoses in fact, into something quite bizarre. There is manifestly no longer any intention whatever of answering the question and it becomes clear that the sole purpose in writing is, as you pointed out earlier, to amuse.

Andrew: That's right, I think I must have got bored with orthodoxy by this stage and decided to write something more 'fringe'.

Spike: 'Fringe' is probably a fairly accurate description of the kind of humour your essay contains. But can I ask you, if I may, was your intention here to amuse yourself only or was there a design to amuse others?

Andrew: I think there must have been, yes; it's reassuring to be laughed at.

Spike: Who were you intending to amuse then: your teacher?

Andrew: Yes; and of course, anyone else you happened to read it. There are generally only two kinds of essays worthy of reading: those that receive a grade 'A' and those that receive a grade 'F'. Essays that receive in-between grades are generally, though not always, pretty boring.

Spike: You made the essay so bad that it was funny, in other words?

Andrew: Something like that, yes.

Spike: Let's take a look at what you actually wrote then. The first sentence of the paragraph is obviously a joke.

Andrew: Why do you say that?

Spike: Isn't it obvious? The thought that an architect might draw up plans for corridors which could be used by snipers is patently ludicrous, is it not?

Andrew: Probably it is.

Spike: And yet despite the seemingly obvious nature of this particular malarkey, your teacher withheld the dreaded pen, except of course from the last few words 'in the most unfortunate ...' which were as usual axed.

Andrew: Perhaps she thought it was a serious suggestion; besides, if she deleted everything of questionable intent there would be no essay left.

Spike: What about the next sentence? You use the word 'subversives' and suggest, as a possible design advantage, that the police might be able to shoot people from their 'corridors'?

Andrew: Personally, I don't consider the idea of the police shooting people to be all that far-fetched.

Spike: But it must, I think, be regarded as rather sensational in an essay ostensibly on the subject of architecture.

Andrew: Possibly.

Spike: Even further deterioration of intent can be observed in the next paragraph. The second sentence contains the word 'yobs', which your teacher circled in red ink.

Andrew: She evidently felt I was being flagrant and was, of course, in no way mistaken.

Spike: The phrase 'undesirable social elements', which you included in the essay to explain the sense of 'yobs', is not immediately offending. But who exactly might qualify as an 'undesirable social element'?

Andrew: It's a very subjective question; to some - skinheads; to some - punks; to others - Conservative MP's.

Spike: I rather think it implies the first and second alternatives more so than the third.

Andrew: In common usage, that's probably true.

Spike: What about your use of the word 'apprehended'; is it just another example of preciosity?

Andrew: Which is in turn an example of itself?

Spike: Quite; but didn't you make particular use of euphuism, for example in the phrase 'eluding the forces of the law' and then again throughout the next paragraph with such words as 'commodities', 'retailed' and 'volumes'.

Andrew: I take your point, though I don't think there was anything particularly ulterior about the use of such words.

Spike: Perhaps not. Now, it was at this point that you elected to, how shall I put it ... interrupt the monotony of continuous prose with a short dialogue?

Andrew: That's right. I thought, as indeed you've just suggested, that it would liven things up a little.

Spike: But introducing speech into a General Studies essay of this type is probably not too good an idea for any of several reasons, is it?

Andrew: It isn't if you want to get any marks; but if getting marks isn't one's primary objective in writing, then I can't see any reason why not.

Spike: It's after your dialogue that your teacher inserted her second comment, 'Point is unworthy of making so much of.' How do you feel about that?

Andrew: I don't agree with the statement at all. I felt then, and still feel, that this particular point is well worth making something of. I must admit, however, that the way in which the point was made was wholly unworthy of the point itself, the point being, as I said, eminently worthy of making.

Spike: The next opinion you expressed is, in my view, an absolute classic and well deserves to be quoted. You wrote: 'If the shopping centre is more than forty stories high it will be too big, I think.'

Andrew: It is something of a classic, I have to agree. It would have been far more engaging, though, had it been written in the Queen's English, or at least some coherent form thereof. It should at the very least have read: 'If the shopping centre were to be more than forty stories high it would be too tall, I think.' As it is, however, the disturbingly ungrammatical combination of present and future tenses in place of the required conditional, necessitated here by the use of 'if', completely destroys any humour it might have had for me and inclines me rather more towards tears of sadness than tears of laughter.

Spike: So, you think that it would have been better to write 'tall' instead of 'big'?

Andrew: Retrospectively, I think so.

Spike: What about your teacher's comment at that point: 'Is this meant seriously?'

Andrew: It was a rhetorical question no doubt.

Spike: No doubt; and at that, let us move on to the last paragraph, the 'grand finale' if you like. Let me ask you first about the forty-nine-word sentence at the beginning of it.

Andrew: The first sentence is perfectly reasonable I think. Anyone failing to recognize the veracity of it would plainly have to be mad.

Spike: Your teacher seems to have objected to the phrase 'absolutely splendid'. Why was that, do you think?

Andrew: I can offer no explanation at all for that. I think it adds a distinctly emphatic flavour to an otherwise dully expressed sentiment.

Spike: Did you think that at the time of writing?

Andrew: I can't remember.

Spike: What about your suggestion that the building you mention 'would look a lot "nicer" if it had some turrets and flags and looked like a medieval castle'?

Andrew: I can do none other than stand by it absolutely. If the building in question were to be built around, even in brick or suitably decorated concrete, it would be far less offensive to the eye than it is at present.

Spike: A serious point then, at least in your opinion, to conclude an otherwise frivolous piece of work?

Andrew: Exactly.

Spike: Thank you very much for talking to me and sharing with me some insights into what I hope my readers will find a thoroughly enjoyable essay on the design of shopping precincts.

Andrew: Thank you.

CHAPTER 4: A LETTER TO 'THE TIMES'

Introduction

A few days after I placed an advertisement in a local newspaper asking for someone to send me a copy of any letter they might have written in preparation for English Language O Level or GCSE, I received a reply from Peter who had written a letter to the 'The Times' newspaper.

The Interview: Part I

Spike: Firstly, thank you very much for sending me your letter; secondly, thank you for agreeing to meet me and discuss it.

Peter: Too bad you're not paying anything.

Spike: Yes, I'm sorry about that. I'm working to ...

Peter: A tight budget; right?

Spike: Right.

Peter: Never mind, I suppose people deserve to know what I think about things. What exactly do you expect me to do anyway?

Spike: Well, what normally happens is ...

Peter: I'm not too bothered about what normally happens: what do you expect me to do?

Spike: Erm ... I want to talk to you about your letter and discuss some of the points arising from it.

Peter: Let's get started then. It's about areas of undeveloped land. They're imaginary areas, that's obvious, but the point is ...

Spike: If I can just stop you there for a second, I normally ...

Peter: I wish you would stop telling me what normally happens; I've told you, I'm not interested in other people.

Spike: That's fine but perhaps we could just read through what you wrote before we begin our ...

Peter: Get that paper out of my face! I wrote the letter; don't you think I know what's in it?

Spike: I'm sure you do but ... erm ... you're quite right: there's no need to read the letter.

Peter: You can't teach an old dog new tricks you know!

Spike: Of course not; but what's ...

Peter: Do you always talk to people about letters?

Spike: Erm ... no. I talk to people about all kinds of school work.

Peter: Such as?

Spike: Answers written during examinations, essays, short stories ... it's important to have some variety.

Peter: It's the spice of youth hostelling!

Spike: What is?

Peter: Variety.

Spike: Is it?

Peter: Of course. I'm greatly surprised you didn't know.

Spike: I've never been Youth Hostelling.

Peter: You've missed a treat. Never been Youth Hostelling - sign of a misspent youth. You know what they say.

Spike: They?

Peter: People ... you know, just people.

Spike: Right.

Peter: Let's get on with talking about my letter now!

Spike: Sure. Let me just ask you first about the question?

Peter: I paraphrased it on the back of the page.

Spike: Ah ... so you did, yes.

Peter: Well, let's get on with it shall we? I've got a train to catch.

Spike: I'm sorry, I didn't real...

Peter: Just kidding: I haven't really. Had you fooled for a minute, didn't I?

Spike: Yes, I must admit I ...

Peter: It's addressed to the editor of 'The Times'.

The Question

Write a letter to 'The Times' expressing your concern that vast areas of wasteland in your area are not being put to better use.

147 Occupation Street,
Newcastle, Staffs.
ST5 11F.

The Editor,
The Times,
71-79 Fleet Street,
London.

3:10:83

Dear Sir,

It is with extreme concern and profound regret that I write to you with the knowledge that great areas of land, in my district, lie undeveloped for lack of money.

In my area there are very many young people who do not know what to do with their time. They seem to walk around aimlessly like a crowd of 'Poyners'. I think, in light of all the wasteland in my area, that some construction could be undertaken by the council to give some interest to young people. I know of a town near here that did undertake such a project. They constructed a beautiful, four storey building. This building, however, was put to poor use, it was called: 'The Baroque Music Appreciation Society House' ... need I say more. One evening last week when an appallingly 'shrill' rendition of Vivaldi's trumpet concerto in C major was taking place, the building was attacked and vandalised horrifically. This type of thing keeps happening in our big cities. I think something should be done about it; don't you?

Yours sincerely,

Peter

Mark and Teacher's Comment

8/20   Hurried and Careless.

The Interview: Part II

Spike: All right, tell me about your letter.

Peter: It's high time we did talk about it: it's been nothing but scraps so far.

Spike: Scraps?

Peter: Scraps of fish and poultry, man: that's all I've had.

Spike: I don't know what you're talking about.

Peter: My letter, sonny, my letter: I was writing letters to 'The Times' when you were still sucking your thumb and wetting your pants.

Spike: I'm sure you were. May I ask you, though, did you write this letter for O Level?

Peter: O Level? It was School Certificate in my day. Things were very different then; not like they are today. I used to eat bread and dripping.

Spike: How nice.

Peter: The doctor came around once, to our house.

Spike: Did he?

Peter: That's right. Do you know what he said to my mother?

Spike: I haven't the vaguest idea.

Peter: He said: 'Don't throw those chicken bones away, they'll make a very nourishing broth for the children.' Did your doctor say that?

Spike: Erm ... no, I don't believe he did.

Peter: Things have changed you see, that's my point. I bet you've never had broth made from chicken bones, have you?

Spike: Erm ... no, I don't ever recall ...

Peter: It's a whole different ball game nowadays - computers, spaceships, videos, compact discs, biscuits ...

Spike: Biscuits?

Peter: No thanks, I've eaten.

Spike: But ...

Peter: Just one of my little jokes, sonny; no need to take offence.

Spike: Perhaps we could get back to your letter to 'The Times'.

Peter: Never had a newspaper as a boy.

Spike: No, no ...

Peter: The problem is with the councils you see; they just won't spend money on urban regeneration.

Spike: You're referring to your letter now?

Peter: Of course, I am; that's what I'm here for, to talk about my letter.

Spike: Go on then, please, you were just about to say something about urban regeneration.

Peter: Just go out for a twenty minute drive and what do you see?

Spike: Erm ...

Peter: I tell you they're everywhere, absolutely bloody everywhere: end of the road, across the street, down where the steel works used to be ... and the pottery, well, that's probably the worst of the lot.

Spike: What exact...

Peter: I blame the councils. I mean, you've got to blame somebody, haven't you? It can't be nobody's fault; somebody's to blame for everything ... or thank, as the case may be. I know it isn't easy these days; but nobody made them stand for office. They're the ones with all the money after all. What do they do with it? That's what I'd like to know. Just look at the cars they drive around in! And what about all those bloody dinners they go to; thieving swine! I hope that answers your question anyway.

Spike: It does, thank you. Can I ask you ...

Peter: That's another point, I'm you glad you raised it. I made it up of course: there was never any such place as the erm... whatever it was ...

Spike: The Baroque Music Appreciation Society House?

Peter: Exactly.

Spike: Why did you make it up?

Peter: I like to make things up. Actually, there's more to it than that: I'm a pathological liar.

Spike: Do you always make things up?

Peter: Always; I just can't help myself. I said 'Enough!' once; but I didn't stop - I couldn't, no more than I could stop breathing and humming tunes to myself at tea time.

Spike: But surely you could get some ...

Peter: No! I couldn't stop even if I wanted to - which of course I don't.

Spike: Why not?

Peter: 'Why not?' You jest Sir, surely? Lying is the greatest narcotic known to man. More soothing than ganja or nicotine or opium; and twice as addictive. Once a man has become used to it he can't ever stop.

Spike: Why not?

Peter: One lie begets another and so it goes on. If I told you I'd been to Moscow, you'd ask what I did there. Of course, I'd have to lie, because I've never been to Moscow. It's a wonderful addiction though, absolutely wonderful; and there are no side effects - no cancer, no drawbacks. Lies are like a fountain swelling up from a deep rock spring: an infinity of anecdotes and stories, a limitless line of people you've met, things you've done, and places you've visited. The pathological liar is never lost for words.

Spike: It's a social thing then?

Peter: Not at all; that's just one of my condition's many advantages. Really it's something you do for yourself; you make up a story and tell a thousand people, they tell other people who later remind you of what you did, or where you went. In the end you believe the story yourself, it becomes part of your history - you develop a memory of something that never happened - you create for yourself a past that really never was.

Spike: But ...

Peter: No, the point is this: the past is gone, never to be seen again. It does not exist; and that's the beauty of it. If you had no friends as a child, what do you tell your children?

Spike: The truth?

Peter: But what is truth? A perception? A reflection of an unreal image? An image of something that no longer exists? The fictional stories you tell your friends, the things you eventually come to believe yourself - how can these be any less real than a thing which is not a thing? For the past is not a thing, it is a thing which does not in fact exist.

Spike: But what are you saying? That lies are ...

Peter: A lie about the past is no less real than the truth about the past; both memory and fiction are equally unreal.

Spike: And the Baroque Music Appreciation Society House?

Peter: I've been there ... yes. I've walked through the great oak doors, up the marble staircase and along the velvet lined balconies. I've sat and listened to the world's greatest virtuosi ...

Spike: All in your dreams?

Peter: Not dreams, sonny: fabrications or some say, lies.

Spike: There is a nuance, then?

Peter: A nuance? No! There is more - much more: this is no mere nuance. The difference is higher than the sky to a daisy; deeper than the sea to a puddle of water. A man experiences dreams; but lies he invents, consciously weaving them from the misery of his life.

Spike: But ...

Peter: The rendition was shrill. I say that in my letter, you know: shrill. That's what it was, all right, no doubt about it. Was that why the building was vandalised? Well ... I would think so: wouldn't you?

Spike: Not because of the Vivaldi, then?

Peter: No, I don't think so; I don't think so at all.

Spike: I must ask you about this expression you used: 'They seem to walk around aimlessly like a crowd of Poyners.' What exactly is a 'Poyner'?

Peter: A certain person I knew in those days.

Spike: What about the mark that ...

Peter: I've written better letters than this one. One letter cannot properly give an indication of a man's literary style; when you're young, you simply don't understand these things.

Spike: What other letters have you ...

Peter: Over a hundred bloody pounds! I don't know how they've got the nerve. Filthy parasites, fascists, that's all they are! It's disgusting: it turns my stomach to think about it!

Spike: What are you ...

Peter: I blame the government. It's totally unjust: totally! The swine should be stopped. Somebody ought to put a stop to their thieving ways! I don't know how they get away with it. I really don't. And the pensioners, I feel sorry for those poor devils, I really do. Sitting in front of it all day with an empty purse. Can you imagine it: having to watch the crap they put on? It's daylight robbery, it is. It's absolutely bloody disgusting how they get away with it.

Spike: Can I just ... what are doing?

Peter: I'll be going now.

Spike: But we were discussing something?

Peter: It's sad, I know; but the time - don't you see the time?

Spike: It's only six ...

Peter: Please, no protestations.

Spike: Very well ... if you have to.

Peter: Which one?

Spike: It's the door on the left.

Peter: Good day.

Spike: Yeah ... thanks ... bye.

CHAPTER 5: A LETTER TO KIEV

<u>Introduction</u>

Following on from my theme in Chapter 4 and resulting from the same advert, I received a second reply worth looking at. This one from a fellow by the name of Robert. Sadly, the interview in this case was brief and had to take place by telephone.

<u>The Interview: Part I</u>

Robert: Hello?

Spike: Hello, is that Robert?

Robert: Yes, it is.

Spike: This is Spike, you sent my one of your O Level English Language exercises.

Robert: Oh yes, that letter I wrote to the Russians.

Spike: That's right, yes. I've read it through and I think it's very interesting. What I'd like to do, if you're agreeable, is meet up and discuss what you wrote in it and why.

Robert: I'm afraid that won't be possible. My company is promoting me to branch manager, unfortunately the branch is in Australia.

Spike: Australia! I see, that is a bit awkward.

Robert: I leave first thing tomorrow morning so ...

Spike: That's perfectly all right, I quite understand. If you could spare me a few minutes though, I could ask you a few questions over the phone?

Robert: Sure, I can spare you a couple of minutes. Fire away.

Spike: At this point in my interviews I usually ask the person I'm interviewing to read through their work with me before we discuss it.

Obviously, that won't be possible in this case, but perhaps you could just imagine you've read it and cast your mind back to what you wrote.

Robert: Sure, no problem.

The Letter

42 Alexander Drive,
Newcastle,
Staffs.

14:2:84.

The Manager,
Mikoyan Co. Ltd.,
Defence Buildings,
Kiev,
U.S.S.R. **(COMMUNIST COUNTRIES DO NOT HAVE LIMITED COMPANIES**!)

Dear Sir,

I am writing to you to ask for your support in a bid to obtain a new school minibus. Furthermore, the lending of your support to our noble cause will promote better East-West relations.

To come down to plain terms, what I and my associates really want from you and your company is some hard cash. I know that that may sound a little bit capitalist and I know you do not approve of that sort of thing but, short of going out and begging from the working classes I do not know how to win some money. If you like, you can fly us a minibus over; we won't mind a bit. You may ask, 'what's in it for us?' Well that is just the kind of reaction I might expect from the capitalist Americans but not from you, 'the guardians of true socialism'. But, to get back to hard facts, you can always include the minibus in your package to get Cruise pulled away.

Well, I think I have said enough nicely, if you don't cough up I will vote Conservative, if you do I'll take a bunch of flowers to Karl Marx's monument. The minibus will bring many advantages to the school and its pupils. The most important, I think, is that we won't have to walk anymore, we won't get wet - look, we'll even paint it bright 'Red'. The pupils of our school will be able to visit exhibitions concerning the steel industry, the pottery industry and other such proletariat delights. Thank you for your co-operation and keep the red flag flying comrade!

Yours sincerely,

Robert

Mark and Teacher's Comment

7/10 (B) A Novel Approach.

The Interview: Part II

Spike: After reading your letter, I was of the same opinion as your teacher: it is without doubt a very novel approach. Can you remember the question?

Robert: Vaguely, yes. It was something like 'write to a local company asking for a donation towards a minibus for your school.'

Spike: But you wrote a letter to Kiev?

Robert: Kiev is local in galactic terms.

Spike: Yes, I suppose it is. Your teacher seemed to like the letter anyway, which is something unusual in itself; most of the people I interview produced works that their respective teachers did not like. I suppose most of the other students in your class must have addressed their letters to, shall I say, more 'normal' companies. What induced you to address yours to a maker of Eastern bloc fighter aircraft?

Robert: I just like being different.

Spike: There's nothing wrong with that I suppose. What about the slip you made in the address itself, writing 'Limited' after Mikoyan Company?

Robert: Yes, I did slip up there. I should have spotted that one.

Spike: The actual content of the letter is fairly straightforward, but it's also a little, shall I say, 'witty' isn't it?

Robert: Yes, I intended it to be. This sort of exercise, writing business letters I mean, can be extremely dull for all concerned.

Spike: So, you were attempting to spice the exercise up a little?

Robert: That's right.

Spike: I think you succeeded.

Robert: Hold on a second ... I think my wife's shouting from upstairs; I'd better go and see what she wants.

Spike: Of course. You don't mind me using your letter and this conversation in my book? I'll only use your first name ...

Robert: I don't mind at all, that's why I sent you the letter. You can use my full name if you like, it's only an old piece of English homework anyway.

Spike: All right, thanks for speaking to me. Enjoy your new life in Australia.

Robert: I will. Good-bye.

Spike: Bye.

CHAPTER 6: ON THE MATTER OF MODERN ARCHITECTURE

Introduction

Some weeks had passed since I had placed the advertisement in a local newspaper asking for someone to send me a copy of any essay which they had written in preparation for General Studies A Level, when I received a reply from Nathan. Curiously and coincidently, during our initial telephone conversation it became clear that Nathan had attended the same school as Andrew (Chapter 3) and had in fact had the same teacher, although they were not in the same class, Nathan being Andrew's junior by two years.

The Interview: Part I

Spike: I'd like to start by asking you when you wrote this essay?

Nathan: I wrote it about erm... about six years ago while I was studying for my A Levels.

Spike: Speaking to someone a few weeks ago, in an interview such as this one, I learned that several schools and colleges actually prepare candidates for General Studies A Level by having them write essays in answer to questions given on previous examination papers.

Nathan: That's right. As we discussed on the phone, it was in answer to a past paper question that I wrote this essay.

Spike: Can you remember the question?

Nathan: Erm ... no, I can't unfortunately: sorry.

Spike: No matter, perhaps I'll be able to find it in a General Studies A Level past papers book.

Nathan: I'm sure you could paraphrase it from the first sentence if not.

Spike: I'm sure I could, yes; though naturally I'd prefer to find the original.

Nathan: Naturally.

Spike: So ... I think we'll move straight on to your essay now; then we can go on to discuss some of the matters arising from it.

Nathan: Sure.

Assignment Question

Unknown.

The Essay.

I think, firstly, that whether or not we consider modern architecture better or worse than traditional architecture is very much a matter of personal opinion. I think probably the main characteristic of modern architecture as opposed to Gothic, Baroque etc. is that it is deliberately plain but not plain in such a way as to be modest but plainer in a such a way as to be bold; as if by being ugly and featureless it catches the eye.

The advent of the modern architecture people has brought particular suffering to church architecture; the great architect Augustus Pugin, when visiting Rome, commented that he disliked Baroque, St. Peter's being built in that style, and preferred the Gothic style for which he is so well noted. But in my opinion, although I prefer Gothic to Baroque, the Baroque style is unquestionably preferable to the sight of Liverpool Metropolitan Cathedral. In my personal opinion the Liverpool Cathedral is the most ugly, disfigured and nauseating monstrosity in the North of England. **(WHY?)** There are many fine examples of Gothic and Baroque architecture such as St. Chad's, Lichfield, Salisbury, St. Paul's, Westminster Abbey and not forgetting Westminster Cathedral, built in an acceptable Byzantine style: it remains only to be said that whatever possessed the architects to disregard the traditional examples and build what they did is beyond all imagination. **(NO, IT IS UP TO YOU TO ANALYSE WHY THEY DID IN ORDER TO ANSWER THE QUESTION.)**

One of the major things with the Liverpool Cathedral is that it does not look a church, I think people have mental images of what cathedrals are supposed to look like and I, for one, feel that the building in question resembles a missile silo more than a cathedral. **(HOW?)** The traditional cathedrals often had figures of saints and crosses, patterned brickwork etc. But not in the modern architectural school - weird shapes and so called 'artistic designs' are all we see. **(WHY?)**   There is a white coloured church in Poland, I can't quite recall where - possibly Gdansk or Cracow - but that is another fine example of ugliness and lack of ecclesiastical character. **(USE EXAMPLES YOU KNOW! NOT ONES YOU CAN'T REMEMBER!!)**

Sometimes the old buildings are knocked down in preference to the new. In the parishes many new churches have been built some of which are horrible, but some are plain in a simple way and not unacceptable. The lack of money, I suppose, at parish level prevents the misfortune of modern architectural design work - if only Liverpool had been so lucky!

Mark and Teacher's Final Comment.

4/20   Your style is too chatty! You must make serious points and argue them logically and not make emotional responses. By restricting yourself to Church architecture you have made the essay harder to write. You have not defined the term 'Modern Architecture'.

The Interview: Part II.

Spike: You start off by suggesting that there exists a high degree of subjectivity in quantifying the relative merits and demerits of Modern Architecture, relative that is, as you yourself state, to traditional architecture. But when you say 'very much a matter of personal opinion' are you saying that the determination is not completely subjective? Is there perhaps some aspect of objectivity?

Nathan: I think the construction resulted from an intention to be euphuistic rather than to express the opinion you've just outlined. It could be argued, though, that a cathedral is architecturally superior to a mud hut.

Spike: When you say, 'it could be argued', on which side of the argument would you place yourself?

Nathan: I think I'd prefer to listen to the argument rather than take sides in it. Questions of subjectivity and objectivity are seldom straightforward.

Spike: But surely with the example you mentioned, of the cathedral and the mud hut, it would be fair to say that the cathedral is architecturally superior.

Nathan: Yes, I agree with you; but having said that I don't think I'd like to argue it rationally.

Spike: It would be easier to argue, though, than the reverse view; wouldn't it?

Nathan: It would depend upon whom you were arguing with.

Spike: Don't you think that it would be possible to rationalise the argument by positing that the mud hut, so to speak, has no architecture?

Nathan: That's a possibility; but again, it would really depend upon whom you were arguing with.

Spike: Let's move on to your next point then. You say that 'the main characteristic of modern architecture is that it is deliberately plain' and then qualify this further by saying that is 'not plain in such a way as to be modest but plainer in a such a way as to be bold; as if by being ugly and featureless it catches the eye'?

Nathan: That's right.

Spike: It's quite an interesting point: do you think it's valid?

Nathan: I think it is valid to a certain extent, yes. But I also think it is necessary to define what one means by the term 'modern architecture', before applying it.

Spike: Your teacher criticized you for not doing that in her final comment, didn't she?

Nathan: Yes, she did; and I think it was a valid criticism. The essay would have been significantly better if I'd done that.

Spike: Do it now then.

Nathan: Sure. I think firstly that it's impossible to talk about modern architecture *en bloc*. In fact, it's almost impossible to talk about anything modern *en bloc*. Take fashion for example: there are many different styles which are current. To which style would the words 'modern fashion' refer? There are simply so many. I think it's the same with architecture. There are so many different forms.

Spike: To narrow the field a little though, isn't it fair to say that modern architecture as a phrase doesn't generally refer to any style of architecture that is current but to a specific style of architecture. For example, if someone were to build a cathedral somewhere in the third world, in say the Byzantine style, it wouldn't really be fair to say that it was a form of modern architecture, or would it?

Nathan: No ... I don't think that it would; and I do take your point. It would not be reasonable to refer to a contemporary architectural style which emulated a previous, as modern.

Spike: Precisely.

Nathan: But having said that, and I do agree with you, I would still maintain that there are differing forms within the broader category of modern architecture.

Spike: Fair enough. Let's talk now for a moment about your contention that some forms of modern architecture are deliberately and, shall I say, emphatically plain. Do you still hold that view?

Nathan: Certainly; I think it's quite obvious when you look at some buildings. There's a perfect example in Newcastle-under-Lyme, Staffordshire.

Spike: Yes, that building's been mentioned before in another interview.

Nathan: Frankly, I'm not at all surprised. It's extremely well known, not to mention well despised, in the area.

Spike: Does that particular building exemplify your argument?

Nathan: Yes, I think it does. In a sense, it is plain. If it wasn't the most dreadfully horrible shade of orange, I think it could fairly be described as very plain indeed.

Spike: From an architectural point of view, that is?

Nathan: Exactly, the exterior is extremely simple and yet it stands out.

Spike: Are there other examples of this same phenomenon in the area?

Nathan: I think there are, yes; though I wouldn't like to cite examples for fear of offending someone.

Spike: That's fair enough; I think the point has been made anyway. Moving on now, to your second paragraph, I notice that you turn to church architecture, and in fact stay with that theme for the remainder of the essay - your teacher commented upon your having done so in fact - was there any particular reason for this?

Nathan: That I dwelt on church architecture you mean?

Spike: Yes.

Nathan: No, not really. I think I probably intended to move on to other forms of architecture later in the essay, but possibly I got side-tracked - I can't honestly remember.

Spike: That's all right. Let's talk about the views you expressed on church architecture then. First, I'd like to ask about the little story you included concerning Augustus Pugin and his trip to Rome; is that factual?

Nathan: I think so, yes.

Spike: Then you don't know that it is?

Nathan: Erm ... no, not for certain. I remember reading it somewhere, I don't recall where, but I've never verified its validity. My teacher never questioned it anyway.

Spike: I noticed that, and it's something that I'd like to expand upon if I may.

Nathan: Sure.

Spike: Let me ask you something: do you think that your teacher might have come across this story about Pugin before?

Nathan: Erm ... I don't know; she may have done. Why do you ask?

Spike: My point is simply this: let's suppose for a moment that your teacher had never come across this story before.

Nathan: OK.

Spike: How would she know if you'd made it up?

Nathan: I'm not sure that I follow you.

Spike: Let me put it like this: suppose that an A Level examiner has to mark a hundred papers. Suppose also that each of those hundred papers contains an essay which in turn contains a small story or anecdote about a relatively obscure person such as Augustus Pugin. Surely it is beyond the realms of possibility that any A Level examiner could possibly be conversant with the life history of every such person ...

Nathan: Are you suggesting that a candidate could invent stories about obscure historical characters to back up his arguments?

Spike: Do you think that could work?

Nathan: Supposing the examiner checked on such stories, though?

Spike: But would someone with a hundred essays to mark in a limited period of time have sufficient time on his hands to do that?

Nathan: I suppose not.

Spike: Surely then, as long as the story *looked* true, the examiner would accept it as such?

Nathan: Yes, yes, I see the point you're making. It's a very subversive idea; but just suppose an examiner were to check on such a story.

Spike: All right, let's suppose for a moment that he did and let's take this story about Pugin as our example.

Nathan: Sure.

Spike: Firstly, it's unlikely that an examiner would have at his disposal a full biography of Pugin – more likely if he did check, he'd just use Wikipedia.

Nathan: True.

Spike: Therefore, his information would be limited and in any case Wikipedia, or similar, tells you what people did – not what they didn't do.

Nathan: Erm ... yes, I suppose that's also true.

Spike: Let's suppose then, for the sake of argument, that in the Wikipedia entry on Pugin, there was no mention at all of him ever having visited Rome. Would the examiner deduct marks?

Nathan: I don't see how he could: a Wikipedia entry generally doesn't contain a person's entire life history unless they're really super famous like Churchill or Napoleon.

Spike: Exactly. The point I'm making is this; surely an examiner would have to give a candidate the benefit of the doubt if unable to find any record of the story.

Nathan: Yes ... I suppose in the final analysis the candidate would have to be given the benefit of the doubt. Let's suppose though, that the Wikipedia entry was relatively detailed and contained an in depth report on the person's life history, surely the absence of such a story would set the alarm bells ringing.

Spike: But the candidate would still be covered. As I just said, even the most detailed biographies and life histories tell of what people did do, not what they didn't do. For example, if you were to read twenty books on the life of Napoleon, I would bet money that none of them would contain the sentence 'Napoleon never went to America'.

Nathan: Yes, I see your point: they tell the reader where people did go, not where they didn't. But surely Napoleon never did go to America?

Spike: Actually, he did, he sailed to New York when he was still a junior officer to visit the new republic.

Nathan: Mmm ... I didn't know that.

Spike: Oh, yes; don't forget the Statue of Liberty was a gift from revolutionary France.

Nathan: Yes, of course; but I'd never made the connection with Napoleon.

Spike: Neither had Napoleon: I just made it up.

Nathan: What's your point here?

Spike: My point is, that although you'd never read anywhere that Napoleon had visited America, you were inclined to believe what I said because it seemed plausible and fitted in with the story about the statue of Liberty which you had heard of or read about before.

Nathan: Yes, it's a very interesting point; and not only interesting, but extremely worrying.

Spike: Why worrying?

Nathan: Because other people could get the same idea and use it to cheat in General Studies examinations.

Spike: Why do you say 'cheat'?

Nathan: It is cheating to write something down that you know to be untrue in order to support a weak argument in an essay.

Spike: But you wrote the story about Pugin in your essay?

Nathan: But I didn't consider the story to be untrue.

Spike: You didn't know that the story was true either though, did you?

Nathan: No, but I can remember having read the story somewhere; I wasn't being dishonest.

Spike: Oh, but you were, because you presented it as fact when you didn't know that it was; and then you used it to illustrate a point that you were making. In order to have been honest, you should have qualified what you said with something like 'I seem to remember reading somewhere ...' or something of that nature.

Nathan: But then I would have drawn the same comment that I drew later on when I mentioned the white church in Poland.

Spike: And you would have lost more marks.

Nathan: Exactly.

Spike: Let's talk about the white church, then. Do you suppose your teacher had ever been to Poland?

Nathan: I'm quite sure she hadn't.

Spike: Suppose, then, instead of writing, 'There is a white coloured church in Poland, I can't quite recall where, possibly Gdansk or Cracow', you'd written, 'there is a large, white church in Gdansk, Poland, dedicated to Saint Stanislaus', do you think your teacher would have written 'Use examples you know! Not ones you can't remember!!'?

Nathan: No, I don't suppose she would; I think she would have passed over it and accepted it as fact, even though it wasn't.

Spike: You say, 'even though it wasn't', but how do you know that there isn't a white church in Gdansk dedicated to Saint Stanislaus?

Nathan: I don't; in fact, for all I know, there very well might be. But surely you aren't suggesting that people adopt this approach in their General Studies A Level exam?

Spike: I don't see why not.

Nathan: Just suppose though, that they have the extreme misfortune of having their paper marked by a former resident of Gdansk, who knows that no such church exists?

Spike: I'm not suggesting that every candidate should invent 'facts' in every essay. If an essay question comes up that a candidate knows sufficient about to answer properly, then by all means let him answer it without resorting to such methods. If, however, a candidate is faced with a choice of, say, six essay titles and knows absolutely nothing about any of them, surely he has a better chance of passing the exam if he makes up some interesting facts and then constructs a well-argued essay around them, than he would have if he just kept waffling on about nothing.

Nathan: But it's still possible, however improbable, that this dishonest, hypothetical candidate could be found out.

Spike: It is possible, yes; and such a course would always be a gamble. There would be absolutely nothing to lose though, because the said candidate couldn't have answered any of the essay questions anyway. There's everything to gain and nothing to lose.

Nathan: I still say it's dishonest.

Spike: It's a dishonest world ... but that's another story. Thank you very much for talking to me.

Nathan: It's been a pleasure.

CHAPTER 7: A LETTER TO MISS GLADSTONE

Introduction

Following on from my theme in Chapters 4 and 5, and resulting from the same advert, I received some weeks after posting the advert, a third reply which piqued my interest due to several somewhat unconventional phraseologies in the schoolwork; the wording of which I immediately related to some Latin works with which I was familiar. These were in stark contrast to the very basic use of English in the covering email. The communication was also unusual in that it was the first one from a female respondent. In fact, the gender split in terms of total respondents was quite interesting in itself (96% Male versus 4% Female) and although beyond the scope of this current work, is no doubt something which deserves further analysis.

The Interview: Part I

Spike: When did you write this letter?

Libby: I wrote it a few months before taking my English GSCE.

Spike: And what was the purpose of writing it?

Libby: To practise writing business letters, that's all.

Spike: Let's have a look at it, then. Afterwards we can discuss some of the points arising from it.

Libby: All right.

Assignment

The original wording has been lost but a reasonable paraphrase would be: "Write a business letter to a Miss Gladstone in response to her advertisement asking for a position as a vocalist in a local band."

The Letter

67 Avington Road,
Newcastle,
Staffs.

22:3:84.

Dear Miss Gladstone,

I am writing to you in answer to the advertisement in the 'Daily Echo' on the 1st August of this year.

Three of my friends and myself formed a pop band just over a year ago. We perform publicly about once or twice a month at third rate night clubs and other establishments of low repute. About a week ago Miss Linda Enbuggar, the singer, arrived at the conclusion that our humble group was not worthy of her profound talents and consequently 'ran off' to Canada with a Methodist minister or perhaps I should say ex-Methodist minister as the previously mentioned young lady did not possess what could be described as Victorian values. There are great and important reasons why I should undertake to fill the absence of a singer in the band. I read that you are an ex-gay swinger and hope that does not mean you have 'gay' tendencies as with a pop band so with everything else, public image is of great importance. You may be interested to know that the band is quite popular in the area and that you will receive about ten or fifteen pounds per performance. If you are interested please contact me at the above address.

Yours sincerely,

Libby

4/10 (B) I presume that this is supposed to a business letter. It should be set out as such with the address of the person addressed top left. A business letter is for information so omit the witticisms please.

The Interview: Part II

Spike: This letter is sociologically and psychologically interesting in so many ways it's actually difficult for me to know where to begin so I guess the best place is to ask, why do you think your teacher only awarded you a mark of four out of ten?

Libby: Because it wasn't a very good business letter probably.

Spike: How did a mark of forty percent translate into a grade B?

Libby: Don't know. Perhaps it was a mistake on his part; perhaps he should have written D.

Spike: Possibly. Turning to another point, then: as this was supposed to be a business letter, why wasn't the address of the person addressed top left?

Libby: I can't remember now; perhaps I forgot to write it in.

Spike: I see. Moving on again, then, let's look now at the content of your letter. What was the purpose of writing 'third rate night clubs and other establishments of low repute'?

Libby: I think that was one of the witticisms the teacher referred to in his final comment.

Spike: Were you trying to be funny then?

Libby: Yeah, I suppose so.

Spike: Do you think you were successful?

Libby: I don't know ... I think it's funny.

Spike: Wouldn't 'only just humorous and even then only slightly' be a far more appropriate description than 'funny'.

Libby: I think it would, yeah.

Spike: What about this person you refer to, Miss Linda Enbuggar? Was she real or only imaginary?

Libby: Why "ONLY" imaginary'?

Spike: Isn't being real, better than being imaginary?

Libby: I don't think there's much difference most days.

Spike: What about it though, was Miss Enbuggar someone you knew at the time or not?

Libby: I made the name up.

Spike: It's an odd name: why not Gladys Smith?

Libby: All names are really the same; they just sound different.

Spike: I see. Why did you enclose the phrase 'ran off' in inverted commas?

Libby: Perhaps it isn't good English.

Spike: 'Perhaps'?

Libby: Yeah, maybe.

Spike: Well, is it or isn't it?

Libby: I don't know really.

Spike: Why didn't you use the word 'elope'?

Libby: I don't know.

Spike: Why Canada?

Libby: It's as good a place as any for fornication and adultery.

Spike: Is it?

Libby: I think so.

Spike: OK, then: yes ... I suppose it is. Why a Methodist minister, though? Why not a priest or a vicar ... or even a rabbi?

Libby: I thought a Methodist minister would sound more shocking.

Spike: Surely a Roman Catholic Bishop would have been more shocking still?

Libby: I think it's already been done in *The Thorn Birds*.

Spike: Why not an albino penguin then?

Libby: I never thought of it.

Spike: Does your letter then, represent a basic lack of imaginative humour?

Libby: Yes, I think it does.

Spike: What about the words 'the ... young lady did not possess what could be described as Victorian values'? Is all that some sort of giant euphemism for the word ...

Libby: Yes, I think it is.

Spike: I see. Moving on again, then, why do you express the hope that Miss Gladstone does not have gay tendencies?

Libby: That would make her a lesbian.

Spike: So?

Libby: Well, would you want a lesbian in your band?

Spike: Mercifully I don't have a band; but if I did, the sexual orientation of its members, would not bother me in the least bit.

Libby: Oh.

Spike: Is that it: 'Oh'?

Libby: I just don't like lesbians.

Spike: Why not?

Libby: They're strange, aren't they?

Spike: I wouldn't say that they were any stranger than anyone else – you know it's the twenty-first century. Considering your age as well, you have some pretty out-dated views – most people would say weird, in fact.

Libby: OK … maybe just the way I was brought up.

Spike: Moving on again then … to the point you make about remuneration. Isn't ten or fifteen pounds a rather meagre sum to pay a member of a rock band?

Libby: Compared with what?

Spike: Compared with the sum that is paid to members of other rock bands?

Libby: Yes but, other rock bands have erm … erm … something that my band will never have.

Spike: Such as?

Libby: They have talent.

Spike: Do you, yourself, lack talent then?

Libby: Yes.

Spike: What a pity.

Libby: It is, yes.

Spike: Can you conjugate the verb 'amare'?

Libby: Pardon me?

Spike: 'Amare' … it's the infinitive of 'to love' in Latin. Can you conjugate its present tense?

Libby: I don't know what you mean.

Spike: You don't know what I mean because you didn't write this letter.

Libby: What?

Spike: It's not your letter; someone else wrote it.

Libby: How do you know that?

Spike: Elementary! If you'd written the letter, then when I asked you to conjugate the verb 'amare' you would have immediately said, 'amo, amas, amat, amamus, amatis, amant', whereas in fact you said, 'pardon me'.

Libby: How does that tell you that I didn't write the letter.

Spike: The letter was clearly written by a Latin scholar.

Libby: How do you know?

Spike: Because it contains two clear allusions to the letters of the younger Pliny.

Libby: Allusions?

Spike: Perhaps I should have said quasi-quotations, for that is clearly what they are. The author of the letter writes: 'There are great and important reasons why I should undertake to fill the absence of a singer in the band.' The younger Pliny writes, in his letter to Romatius Firmus: 'There are great and important reasons why I should undertake to increase your rank.' Now tell me that the person who wrote this letter was not a student of Pliny.

Libby: I don't know.

Spike: The author of this letter also writes, '... as with a pop band so with everything else ...' – it's very curious and antiquated phraseology.

Libby: So?

Spike: The younger Pliny wrote, in his excellent and incisive letter to Sosius Senecio, '... as with the duty of listening so with everything else ...' Now, how can you possibly argue with such clear evidence?

Libby: All right, I admit it: it's not my letter, I didn't write it.

Spike: Who did?

Libby: A friend, a former colleague ... but she's dead.

Spike: Dead?

Libby: Yes.

Spike: I See ... well ... I suppose if she's dead then she won't object to my including her letter in my book will she?

Libby: No ... I suppose not.

Spike: Thank you very much for talking to me, then. It's been most interesting.

Libby: Thanks too ... it was interesting. Sorry for lying about the letter.

Spike: No apologies needed. I will be writing another book soon ... would you be willing to be interviewed again?

Libby: What's it about?

Spike: Would it make a difference to your answer?

Libby: No ... you can call me, I'll do it.

Spike: Thanks.

Libby: Bye then.

CHAPTER 8: ELGAR AND CRICKET

Introduction

Following the second appearance of my newspaper advertisement for A Level General Studies essays, Natalie emailed me attaching a scanned copy of an essay she had written shortly before her final exam. I wrote back to her, thanking her for the essay and inviting her to meet with me to discuss some of the points she had raised in it. Within the week, I received a second email, declining my invitation to meet, but nevertheless authorising me to use her essay in my book.

Although it was my original intention not to include a piece of work without an interview, I felt in this particular case that an exception to that rule would be in order. As both of Natalie's emails were very brief and to the point, I can offer my readers no further information on the essay other than that which the essay, itself, contains. I understand that the question came from an A Level past paper.

The Exam Question

"Giving examples from at least two sports, analyse and discuss how far it is appropriate to regard sport as a serious part of culture, analogous to the arts."

The Essay

In the modern world the discreet national cultures of the past have been seriously undermined as the peoples and cultures of previously distant lands have been brought closer together. The cultures of various peoples and nations have been mingled together meaning that today a sport or art form is no longer as indicative of its national origin as perhaps it would have been a hundred or so years ago. However, it may still be both possible and appropriate to draw an analogy between sport and art as a serious part of culture.

Is snooker, for example, as serious an expression of the English culture as, for example, the music of Edward Elgar? Certainly, I think, most people would agree that in spite of the fact that Elgar's music is performed all over the world it retains the feeling and character of something both typically and perfectly reminiscent of England. Although snooker may still be considered as essentially an English game, does it express the same typically English culture, typically English way of life, as the previous example? Perhaps it is unfair to compare the work of an individual to an activity of many, but I feel it is unavoidable to do so. Sport and art do not occupy the same place in a national or chronological culture, I do not think they should have to compete for which is to represent the character of the culture or society; however, if one of them is to be more indicative, or one of them is to be a more serious part of culture than the other, then I think it is justifiable to say that the arts represent a more serious part of culture than does sport. And I think that this is so for the following reasons.

Most national and cultural art forms are the work of individuals working in an individual way, apart from certain styles which exist, and which have arisen and continued to flourish in a nation. Some art forms, such as Gothic architecture for example, exist in several countries and yet they are nevertheless indicative of one culture. The people of France who built Gothic churches and the people of England who built Gothic churches did so as part of the same Norman culture, they lived in more or less the same sort of houses, wore the same clothes etc. Later on, Europe adopted a style of Baroque art. Again, the people who painted Baroque pictures and constructed Baroque buildings belonged to almost identical cultures, wearing same clothes, doing same jobs, etc..

If, however, you compare the painting of Baroque pictures to the playing of cricket you can see that the people who painted the Baroque pictures were all of the same culture whereas the people who play cricket are all of different cultures.

The people of Germany, France and Italy having the same background and culture and displaying the Baroque style compared to the people of India, a Hindu and third world country; Pakistan, a Moslem and third world country and England, a Christian country. All playing the same game and yet all having a completely different background and culture.

From this it can be seen that one art form is almost always represented by one culture whereas one sport is represented by many different cultures. This shows that art is a more serious and discreet part of culture than is sport.

Teacher's Comment.

I think you have misunderstood the question.

Spike's Comment

It's a pity that this lady declined to be interviewed as I shall now remain eternally perplexed by the words, "If ... you compare the painting of Baroque pictures to the playing of cricket ...". I do not believe that I have ever met anyone who has either entertained or even considered entertaining such a comparison and even if I live to ripe old age I never will. I wonder also why no grade was given?

CHAPTER 9: SHORT STORIES

Introduction

A few days after I placed an advertisement in a local newspaper asking for someone to send me a copy of any short story which they had written in preparation for English Language O Level or GCSE and for which, contrarily, such person had received a high mark, I received a reply from Hugo. Hugo in fact sent over five such short stories, two of which are featured here.

The Interview: Part I

Spike: Well, first of all I'd like to thank you for sending me so many pieces of work. I've chosen the two I told you on the phone - both pieces of English Language class work, I believe?

Hugo: Yes, I did them during a lesson.

Spike: How come you did this work in class, most of the people I've interviewed did this kind of thing at home.

Hugo: Well, I should have done them at home, but I was always far too busy to bother about homework, so I did them in class.

Spike: And by doing so, you didn't have any homework?

Hugo: That's right.

Spike: That's fine, but perhaps you could clear something up for me?

Hugo: Sure.

Spike: If you did your homework during lesson time, what happened to your class work?

Hugo: Let me explain the system to you. As preparation for our English Language exam, we had to follow some silly book, I can't remember what is was called but it really sucked ...

Spike: Sucked?

Hugo: That's right, it sucked; but anyway, during every lesson we had to do one of the exercises from the book. Now, each exercise consisted of two parts: firstly, a comprehension and secondly, a creative piece ...

Spike: Such as the two you sent to me?

Hugo: That's right. Now, what happened was this: we got to the lesson and the teacher would ask someone to read out the relevant short passage from the book. After that, we had about half an hour to answer say fifteen or twenty questions on the passage, to see if we understood it. Then for homework, we had to do the creative piece.

Spike: Right, so you decided to do the creative piece in class and leave the comprehension for homework?

Hugo: No, I decided not to do the comprehension at all and then copy it from somebody at the end of the lesson, that way I could do my creative piece in class and not have any homework.

Spike: So, you're telling me that you copied the work from your schoolmates that you were supposed to do in the lesson?

Hugo: That's right.

Spike: But why?

Hugo: Why? Are you kidding? Haven't you ever done one of those comprehensions? They're mind-numbingly boring, I can tell you - totally coma-inducing.

Spike: But how did you get away with it? Weren't you ever caught out by the teacher?

Hugo: Never.

Spike: Your teacher must have been pretty oblivious.

Hugo: No, not really: he was quite on the ball. Besides, I did exactly the same thing in no end of other subjects.

Spike: How come you never got found out though? Your answers must have been the same as the person you copied from?

Hugo: Of course not! I always used the "Alternating Source, Order and Thesaurus Method".

Spike: The what?

Hugo: The Alternating Source, Order and Thesaurus method.

Spike: Go on, please; I'm baffled.

Hugo: You want me to explain what it's all about?

Spike: If you would.

Hugo: All right. The first thing you have to do is borrow the work of two people who don't sit together; that way their answers won't be the same, i.e. they won't have copied from each other, and they won't have made the same mistakes. Then, you copy the answer to the first question from one, the second question from the other, the third question from the first one again, and so on. That's the alternating source part. Also, though, while you're copying, you change the order of the sentence. For example, suppose the comprehension passage is about a cat called Felix.

Spike: OK.

Hugo: Then, say for example, one of the questions was: 'Why was Felix often given water instead of milk?' The person from whom you were copying might have written: 'Felix was given water instead of milk because he often misbehaved', so you'd write: 'Felix often misbehaved and as a result was frequently given water instead of milk'. So, you just change the order of the words, you see?

Spike: Yes, I see what you mean; but what about the last part?

Hugo: You mean the thesaurus part?

Spike: Yes.

Hugo: Most of the time it can be dispensed with, but say for example the teacher was suspicious, then you could use the thesaurus method to cover the trail even better. Instead of changing 'Felix was given water instead of milk because he often misbehaved' to 'Felix often misbehaved and as a result was frequently given water instead of milk' you'd change it to 'Felix could at times become quite unruly; his milk was replaced by water when this happened, to encourage him to mend his ways'. As you can see, 'misbehaved' has given way to 'unruly'; and the words 'instead' and 'often' no longer appear at all.

Spike: It seems like rather a lot of trouble?

Hugo: It is in a way, but after a few months of practice it becomes almost second nature; and anyway, it's far less time consuming than going through the passage over and over again looking for the answers.

Spike: I take your point. Now I think we'll have a look at one of your pieces. I'd like to begin with the one entitled 'Return from Space', which I believe takes the form of a short story.

Hugo: That's right, it's only a few hundred words - easily reeled off in a thirty minutes lesson.

Spike: Right. Can you remember what the assignment asked you do?

Hugo: The question? Yes, it was something along the lines ...

Assignment

Imagine you bump into an old friend whom you have not seen in many years. Write a creative piece imaging the dialogue which might occur between you and also describe the ways in which your friend may have changed since you last met him or her.

'Return from Space.'

A few years ago, a good friend of mine went away on a mission to the moon. I saw him again on a morning last week and he really had changed a lot. Here is the dialogue which occurred between us on this happy occasion.

'Fred! Fred! It is Fred, isn't it?' I shouted across the street.

'Oh, by George, old fellow, nice to see you,' he replied scurrying across the street to meet me. He had changed awfully.

'My goodness, Fred, haven't you got a lot of legs; and look at that horn, by the roast!'

'Well, on the moon everybody has to do so much walking all over the place and well, two legs simply aren't enough. I've got six now you know, about this horn - well it was a funny state of affairs, no doubt about it. I was walking along the high street, this is at the Tycho Crater City, and a mouse came up to me and hit me over the head. At the time I thought nothing of it but a bit later when I was shaving I noticed a horn protruding from my head. Well naturally I went straight to the doctor's surgery, he said that on the moon bumps didn't cause lumps - they caused horns and in a few days it would go away so I expect by Friday it will be gone.'

'Well then, everything is fine with you?'

'Oh yes everything's really top class old man, not a problem I could mention, old boy.'

'That's good. Well, I'll be seeing you then. Good bye!'

'Good bye, old chap!'

At that he scuttled off into the distance, but his legs must have got carried away because the next time I saw him he was in a wheelchair legless. I never could understand that silly man; I always maintained he was deranged and now I know for sure.

Mark and Teacher's Comment

17/20   Good.

The Interview: Part II

Spike: It's a rather unusual piece of work.

Hugo: Why do you say that?

Spike: Isn't it obvious?

Hugo: Not to me.

Spike: Well, for a start, don't you find the subject matter somewhat extraordinary?

Hugo: No.

Spike: I see. Where did you get your idea though? Surely the questioner's intention was that you should write something more, shall I say, down to earth. Say, about someone returning from working in the US or Europe or something.

Hugo: I don't see why: my story's as good as any. There are a multitude of ways to answer such a question.

Spike: But isn't it true that there are really only two principal kinds of change possible?

Hugo: True indeed: the physiological and the psychological.

Spike: Would you care to expand on those?

Hugo: I would, yes. I deal in my excellent story with the physiological dimension. Of course, it was possible, and would no doubt have been most interesting to have dealt with the psychological. For example: a former friend could have returned from the United States, to use your example, and been found to be extremely materialistic. My friend could have been a former member of the Communist Party and been converted, or should I say - subverted, to Republicanism.

Spike: Of course; but how would you have brought that out in such a piece as the one you wrote?

Hugo: My friend could have greeted me with the words: 'I'm on a hundred grand a year net, how about you?' or he could have said 'I'm a CEO now; what are you?'

Spike: Have you ever had that experience yourself?

Hugo: Yes, I speak from experience. Whenever I meet former colleagues or school associates, they either avoid speaking to me altogether or instantly tell me what good jobs they have and how much they're earning.

Spike: Does that bother you?

Hugo: Inordinately.

Spike: Why?

Hugo: Firstly, a person's value cannot be determined by how much he is paid or what job he does; and in those very few cases where it sometimes can, it most commonly does so perversely.

Spike: I agree with your first point entirely; but what do you mean when you say, 'in those very few cases where it sometimes can, it most commonly does so perversely'?

Hugo: I'm glad you asked me that. It often happens that the 'better' the job a person has, the stupider the person is.

Spike: Often?

Hugo: There are always exceptions to every rule.

Spike: What do you do, purely as a matter of contextual interest?

Hugo: I sweep up leaves.

Spike: And in summer and spring?

Hugo: Litter ... mostly litter.

Spike: I see.

Hugo: Returning to what I was saying then, apart from the psychological differences possible, there is also the possibility of physiological difference.

Spike: Surely though, physiological difference is more readily understood as: going grey, developing facial lines and wrinkles, growing a beard?

Hugo: 'More readily understood' implies perception, in which case I must say that it all very much depends on who it is that is doing the perceiving.

Spike: I take your point; but having a friend turn into a centipede-unicorn mutant is surely excessive for the purposes of English Language GCSE.

Hugo: It depends upon one's definition of excessive: I can only say that I don't personally find it so.

Spike: Fair enough. Perhaps we can take a look at the text itself now.

Hugo: By all means.

Spike: Your character, Fred, says that everybody has to do a lot of walking on the moon; but where do you suppose these people walk to?

Hugo: I don't suppose; I know.

Spike: Perhaps you could tell me?

Hugo: People walk to the craters and back.

Spike: I see ...

Hugo: And the seas, the marshes and the lakes.

Spike: I was unaware of the existence of such places.

Hugo: Oh yes, there are copious such places.

Spike: What's all this about the Tycho Crater City?

Hugo: It's a city built within the Tycho Crater.

Spike: Isn't it dangerous to build cities in craters?

Hugo: No more dangerous than living in Moss Side.

Spike: Right. Moving on to a physiological question, why do bumps result in horns on the moon; surely there's no scientific reason why it should be so?

Hugo: No, I don't believe there is.

Spike: It's a purely fictional device then?

Hugo: I'm afraid so.

Spike: Just one last point then, before we move on to your next story ... in the last sentence you say: 'I never could understand that silly man; I always maintained he was deranged and now I know for sure'. Placing yourself in the position of the fictional narrator of the tale, how is it that you now 'know for sure'?

Hugo: I'm not sure, erm ...

Spike: You see, from what you wrote it appears that Fred is proved deranged by losing his legs and making use of a wheelchair?

Hugo: Yes, yes, that is how it seems.

Spike: Is it by virtue of those reasons then, that Fred is proved deranged.

Hugo: In the context of the story, I think it is, yes. Though I have to say that the circumstances described prove no such thing.

Spike: And at that, let us move on to your second story.

Assignment

Write a creative piece of not more than 500 words ending with the words 'I shall never be superstitious again'.

Night Life

As I was walking down a dark country lane in the dead of night I heard something behind me. I turned around quickly and there, about twelve miles down the road, was a small black thing moving towards me.

'I must have good hearing!' I said to myself. Then a man, robed entirely in black, jumped out of the hedgerow and stood before me.

'But you were just over there!' I said to him.

'I know,' said he, 'I'm a fast walker: no doubt about it.' We walked a little further on and then we began to converse with each other.

'My name's Nebb Yunot,' I said, 'what's yours?'

'Dracula Smith. I'm a vampire from Leeds and I'm going to kill you, little man.'

'I see, that's not very nice of you, is it? You can't anyway,' I replied.

'Why not?' he asked.

'Because I've got a cross in my pocket,' I pronounced, very pleased with myself.

'That cross doesn't bother me,' he replied, 'I'm a very religious vampire, in fact I'm a Catholic.'

'Well this is an Anglican cross,' I said, waiting to see what his comeback would be.

'That doesn't bother me either because I strongly support Christian unity and the ecumenical movement. So there!'

'O.K.,' I said, 'I've got some garlic as well.'

'I've got a cold!' he replied, 'and a blocked nose.'

'Begone!' I cried.

'No. I'm going to kill you now,' he attested.

'I'm going to kill you! I've got a stake and mallet in my bag, I've just been camping you see.' I thought I had him now.

'That can't hurt me,' he said. By now I was angry.

'And why not?' I screamed. He told me:

'Because I've got a breast plate under my three piece suit. You can't hammer your stake through there, old top!'

'Ha! Ha!' I exclaimed, 'But I've got a pint of holy water in my hip pocket.' He looked startled and said,

'It will take more than that to melt me I assure you.'

'Soulless exhibitionist!' I cried.

'I'm going to cut your legs off and your arms. Then I'm going to tie you up and sew your left leg into your right arm socket, your right leg into your left leg socket, your left arm into your right arm socket and your right arm into your right leg socket,' he said smiling.

'I say!' I said, ' that's not fair play you know, are you sure you're a Catholic? What happened to Christian charity? Don't you have sins where you come from?'

'O.K.,' said he, 'I'm going to recite a poem for you.'

'No thanks!' I said. But for his presence I would have been quite happy, and he proceeded to recite his poem.

'Every week on Saturday,

All the cats come out to play,

They play on the lawn so very quickly,

But not on the road because it's prickly,

They don't go home to have their dinner,

Except to poison the latest winner,

All the losers play him a tune,

By hitting his head with a massive spoon.'

Then I was astonished by the excellence of his poetry, I clapped loudly. Then he went away, and he did not come back again.

'Good-day!' I shouted but he was gone into the night. I told my father and mother - they disinherited me. I told my boss - he sacked me. I told my wife - she divorced me. No! I will never be superstitious again.

Mark and Teacher's Comment

18/20   Most Surrealistic! Do you read Ray Bradbury?

The Interview: Part III

Spike: An astonishing piece of work.

Hugo: Thank you.

Spike: So many layers of meaning and allusion, quite remarkable in fact. Allow me to start by asking you about the first sentence: was what you wrote here influenced at all by your reading of Coleridge.

Hugo: I don't recall telling you that I'd read any Coleridge, but in fact you're quite right: I think the first sentence does allude to the Rime of the Ancient Mariner.

Spike: There are several pieces of light humour in the story, such as your exclamation on the deftness of your hearing; how do you think they influenced the mark you received?

Hugo: They seem to have been appreciated by my teacher; I think that view is clearly supported by the mark I received.

Spike: Like your first story, this one could be considered to constitute a slightly off-beat approach. Do you think the piece is objectively good?

Hugo: Erm ...

Spike: I suppose what I'm asking is: would you have received such a high mark from another teacher?

Hugo: Difficult to say, really.

Spike: Suppose you'd written the story in French for example, and presented it to your French teacher?

Hugo: I would have received a considerably lower mark; but then my French wasn't very good.

Spike: You don't think that the content would have been penalised, then?

Hugo: No, I don't think so: why should it have been?

Spike: Moving on then, your teacher described your work as surrealistic; why do you think he used that word rather than 'surreal', and what significance, if any, do you think there was in his usage?

Hugo: I'm not terribly sure there's actually a lot of difference in common English usage, though I take your point; had our roles been reversed I would probably have used 'surreal'.

Spike: Why?

Hugo: In my view, 'surreal' would have been safer: it can more readily be seen as a synonym for, say, 'dreamlike'. 'Surrealism', to my mind, suggests something far more systematic; it suggests that the piece actually belongs, or perhaps I should say - stems from, the Surrealist movement.

Spike: Your teacher posed the question: 'Do you read Ray Bradbury?'

Hugo: That's right.

Spike: Well? Do you, or did you?

Hugo: No, I've never read anything by him.

Spike: That clears that up then. Moving back to the text itself now, what significance does the name 'Nebb Yunot' have? It seems rather odd to me.

Hugo: It's a simple degeneration of 'Tony Benn' spelt backwards.

Spike: For what reason?

Hugo: None at all.

Spike: What about the Vampire's claim to be Catholic? Isn't that also rather odd?

Hugo: I don't think so, no. Vampires are generally dead, I should say 'undead', people. Such people may or may not have been Catholics while they were alive. Statistically speaking, it seems likely that some of them were Catholics - especially the ones from Poland - presumably some vampires may not wish to abandon the habits of a lifetime after becoming undead.

Spike: Presumably not. But what about the inefficacy of all the traditional tools of the vampire hunter? Is their uselessness in the face of this particular vampire some sort of metaphor?

Hugo: I don't think so, no. At least that was not my intention at the time; though of course it may be possible to assign some sort of metaphor, retrospectively.

Spike: What kind of metaphor do you think might be appropriate?

Hugo: I'd have to think about that one.

Spike: Perhaps we could return to the point later on then. Turning now to the poem that appears towards the end of your story, can I ask you firstly, did you write it yourself?

Hugo: Yes.

Spike: Why is it that you wrote, then: 'I was amazed at the excellence of his poetry'?

Hugo: Placing myself in the position of the fictional narrator, I was amazed by its excellence.

Spike: That's odd.

Hugo: For what reason?

Spike: The poetry isn't excellent.

Hugo: Erm ... perhaps not when judged conventionally against the benchmarks of Shelley and Wordsworth, but it does possess a certain erm ... je ne sais quoi.

Spike: You may not know what, but I most certainly do; in my view there's no way the poem can be described as excellent - in fact, it can only just be described as a poem.

Hugo: Nevertheless, I was amazed at its excellence and I did clap loudly.

Spike: In appreciation of your own poetry?

Hugo: Precisely: I've always been my best audience.

Spike: I see. Moving on now to one last point, why did you include the sentence about the rearrangement of your limbs? It doesn't seem to tessellate ... fit together with the rest of the dialogue, in other words.

Hugo: I think I'd have to agree with you on that point. I'm not really sure why I included it.

Spike: The net result of the operation, if it were to be carried out, would be rather odd I think. One cannot easily escape the fact that it would leave your left arm socket completely vacant and result in there being two limbs emanating from your right arm socket.

Hugo: Yes, I see your point; there's something wrong somewhere.

Spike: Indeed. One last point on this issue ...

Hugo: Go on.

Spike: You have your vampire say to your fictional self: 'I'm going to cut your legs off and your arms. Then I'm going to tie you up ...' I have to ask you: what exactly is there left to be tied up?

Hugo: Ah, yes, I see your point; another small error. Putting you off for a moment though, something's just come to me regarding the inefficacy metaphor we were discussing earlier.

Spike: Please?

Hugo: The inefficacy of the traditional vampire repellents could be seen as a metaphor for the lone traveller's inability to repel violent attack.

Spike: Well, thank you very much for that: it's very interesting.

Hugo: Thank you.

Spike: And thank you for speaking to me about your work.

Hugo: Thank you.

CHAPTER 10: MUSEUMS TODAY

Introduction

For whatever reason, I had developed a curious and yet abiding fascination with essays written in preparation for General Studies A Level and accordingly decided to place a third advertisement for the same. I received a reply from Rupert who had written what I considered to be an interesting piece regarding museums.

The Interview: Part I

Spike: Firstly, thank you for agreeing to speak to me. Secondly, tell me about the context of the essay you sent me.

Rupert: I wrote it while preparing for my General Studies A Level as you already know. It was, as I recall, done as homework. It took about an hour to write ... I think that's about it.

Spike: And it was done while you were in the upper sixth, i.e. the year immediately preceding the final exam?

Rupert: It was.

Spike: Fine. Let's take a look at it then.

Rupert: OK.

Essay Question

Museums today are more popular than they have ever been, largely because techniques of display and presentation have been so much improved. Comment upon and discuss.

I would consider the comment, 'Museums today are more popular than they have ever been, largely because techniques of display and presentation have been so much improved', as true to a lesser extent than other factors.

I think that the reason for museums being more popular today than they have been previously is the present social framework of society, leading to an interest in art and science amongst the working-class people instead of just amongst the upper and middle class. During the Victorian period the museum began its rise; a new interest in the past emerged although the majority of the working-class were still too fatigued by a laborious existence to be interested in learning of any form. Indeed, the old social order openly discouraged any learning, any interest in science and art amongst the working-class 'to keep them down'. The end of the last century marked the end or at least the beginning of it, of the old social order. A growing awareness of learning and education evolved and after the Great War a new realisation of the past and indeed contemporary achievement emerged. In conclusion then, the latent interest of the working class in museums became specific and this century marked a new age of enlightenment cutting straight through the differences of social fabric.

Of course, the methods of presentation in museums have undoubtedly improved over the past years, departing from a 'sparse scattering of ancient artefacts in glass boxes' to a more vivacious display that looks to some extent more realistic and helps to integrate the spectator into the past environment. However, I personally consider the improvement in presentation a result of the new interest and not its cause but, having said that, it must be conceded that many people have been attracted by the 'changing face' of museum presentation.

Probably the museum with which I am best acquainted is the one at Hanley, which I have been to twice, once to have a look at and once to get out of the weather. I don't really like the museum displays although many are well presented and fully documented for the visitor's information. I prefer science museums because they offer information of a potentially greater practical application and interest than museums that deal only with the past. I find looking at how people lived, especially in the inner-cities where there was much poverty, extremely dull and depressing. There are, of course, many people who are interested in such things and find great pleasure in learning about them.

One other type of museum worthy of mention is the industrial museum: mining museums, railway museums etc. I have not visited any such places because I am not very interested in mining, railways or such industrial relics. **(DO NOT EMPHASIZE YOUR OWN RESTRICTED INTERESTS! THIS SHOWS A CLOSED MIND!!)**

In concluding this essay, therefore, I would say that the renewed interest in museums is due mainly to socially orientated factors but partly, only, due to the improvement of the presentation. Indeed, I would say the latter factor is a consequence of the former.

Grade Awarded and Teacher's Comment

Grade D.

Generally, a good use of language. Why not analyse the improvements in scientific museums? This would have made for a more factually based essay and a less 'woolly' essay on your opinions!

The Interview: Part II

Spike: Reading over what you wrote in this essay, I get the impression that it was initially intended quite seriously. There are no hints of humour in the first two paragraphs at all. In the third paragraph, there is only one phrase that could reasonably be deemed in any way jocund.

Rupert: Yes. I think it probably was intended seriously ... at first, as you say. Reading over it myself, just now, I thought it was actually rather good.

Spike: I wouldn't quite go that far myself, but you mean as regards the points you raised?

Rupert: Yes.

Spike: Sure; and I'd like to come to that later. For the moment though, I want to pursue another point.

Rupert: OK.

Spike: It is not, in my view at least, until the fourth paragraph of the essay that one of the only two marginally facetious statements appears.

Rupert: Let me see ... yeah, I guess that's true but ...

Spike: You see, at this point it will probably seem a little odd to my readers that I've chosen to include this particular essay in my anthology at all.

Rupert: How so?

Spike: The main purpose of the anthology was to present ridiculous pieces of semi-English prose that were intended to be amusing.

Rupert: Why did you choose my essay then? And ask to speak to me? According to you, it only has two ...

Spike: Yes, only two, and even then not particularly, amusing expressions.

Rupert: So, why did you choose it?

Spike: During the course of my research I seem to have developed something of an interest into the differing approaches that exist towards the answering of General Studies essay questions. In my view, your essay illustrates just such an approach.

Rupert: It does?

Spike: Yes, I believe so. You see, the more astute reader will no doubt have already noticed a somewhat curious facet of this essay.

Rupert: Which is?

Spike: Which is: that we have here an essay of almost five hundred words, ostensibly on the subject of museums, which contains virtually not one single fact about museums worthy of that description. How cunningly you thought this actuality had been disguised, and yet how easily the deficiency was spotted by your teacher.

Rupert: And so; it seems that you are something of an astute observer of essays yourself.

Spike: Practise makes perfect, as someone once said. I believe that a more detailed examination of your text is in order. Firstly, I must ask you this: what was the purpose of your essay?

Rupert: An opinion is expressed in the first sentence, namely: 'Museums today are more popular than they have ever been, largely because techniques of display and presentation have been so much improved.' The purpose of my essay was to comment upon that opinion and to discuss it .

Spike: Discuss it with whom?

Rupert: With myself, I guess.

Spike: How very curious.

Rupert: For the benefit of those not acquainted with General Studies, allow me to say that this type of question is highly typical of those appearing on A Level examination papers. Opinions are frequently expressed and then customarily followed by such appendices as 'Comment upon and discuss' - or something of like form.

Spike: And so, you proceeded to comment upon the said opinion and discuss it with yourself?

Rupert: Exactly.

Spike: Tell me, as a matter of interest ... no, forgive me: it is more than idle curiosity that prompts my question - were you instructed to write this particular essay, or did you select it yourself, from several alternatives?

Rupert: I chose it myself ... I think from a selection of six. As you know, there is generally a choice on the essay sections of about that number.

Spike: It is here that a point of interest arises, then. How odd that you should have chosen to answer a question on museums and the various methods of display therein.

Rupert: Why do you think it odd?

Spike: Clearly, you know very little about museums. You wouldn't happen to remember any of the alternative essay questions?

Rupert: I'm afraid not; but I know what you're getting at and you're absolutely right.

Spike: Tell my then, why did you choose the essay on museums?

Rupert: Because I felt that that was the one I could answer best.

Spike: In spite of the fact you knew virtually nothing about museums?

Rupert: Not in spite of that fact; because of it.

Spike: Would you care to elaborate?

Rupert: I would. As you have already observed, I knew then, and in fact know now, very little about museums.

Spike: Surely such a state of ignorance is by no means conducive to the composition of a 'factually based essay'. You had by your own admission, only visited your local museum twice.

Rupert: I had not in fact, contrary to my claim, visited the museum only twice; my father has something of a predilection for such nostalgia and I had been to the museum several times with him and my brother. Nor did the occasions on which I visited the museum turn out to be as thoroughly tedious experiences as I suggested. There were, as I recall, some interesting exhibits; although these were by no means numerous and were by far outnumbered by a lot of jumble sale items.

Spike: Jumble sale items?

Rupert: I don't know what else you'd call them; old tins and spoons, pieces of broken pottery et cetera.

Spike: Was it true that you ran into the museum one day to escape from a sudden shower?

Rupert: Perfectly true. I remember the occasion well.

Spike: Did you look at anything while you were there?

Rupert: I recall walking briefly around the art exhibition, yes.

Spike: What did you make of it?

Rupert: It was pitiful.

Spike: I see ... getting back to the matter in hand, then: it is clearly the case that you did not possess the necessary raw materials with which to construct a 'factually based essay'?

Rupert: I did not possess them, and I make no bones about it. I was, and am, ignorant of the high science which deals with methods of display in museums.

Spike: Why write an essay on that subject then?

Rupert: You know why already, don't you? That's why you chose my essay.

Spike: I do know, yes; and that is why I chose your essay ... but tell me anyway, if you wouldn't mind.

Rupert: Very well then. It was my policy at that time, and a wholly laudable one if I may be permitted to say so ...

Spike: You may say whatever you like.

Rupert: Most gracious ... it was my policy to select from the choice of six, in the absence of an essay title on a subject that I knew enough about to write competently, the essay question on the subject I knew least about.

Spike: And this policy was, in contrast to its initial appearance, one of great logic, wasn't it?

Rupert: It was indeed. You see, if a question had been set on a subject in which I was well versed, then that was all very well and good and I would answer it accordingly. It often happened, however, that from the six questions on offer there was not even one on an issue which I knew enough about to write anything like a good essay. Of course, when this was the case, there were invariably two or three I had some knowledge of, but not a great deal.

Spike: So why did you choose to write essays on subjects that you knew virtually nothing about?

Rupert: Perhaps the matter would benefit from the use of an example. Let us consider, then, a hypothetical situation in which I can choose between two essay questions: one on glass vases and one on ... erm ... the history of American car production.

Spike: Very well.

Rupert: Now, if I were to choose the question on American car production, I would no doubt have occasion to re-tell the well-known anecdote about how you can have any colour you like, so long as it's black. I could also mention that Henry Ford invented the production line.

Spike: Did he?

Rupert: You're suggesting he didn't?

Spike: I don't know; do you?

Rupert: I think he did.

Spike: But you're not certain?

Rupert: Erm ... no, I'm not certain; and that's exactly the point I'm making. If I'd chosen to answer the question on glass vases, the matter of who had invented the production line would never have arisen.

Spike: Similarly, if, as happened to another person I interviewed, you were to answer a question on modern architecture, you might well be tempted to mention that there is an ugly white church somewhere in Poland. If you were to write down this information in an essay, the person who marked your essay could well consider you ignorant for not knowing the precise location of the said church ... even though the information is not exactly common knowledge. If, on the other hand, you knew absolutely nothing about the ugly white church in Poland, then you could not mention it in your essay, the question of its location would never arise, and thus you would not appear ignorant.

Rupert: Yes, that's exactly it. If I left the question on modern architecture well alone and tried to answer the question on glass vases, due to the fact I know absolutely nothing about glass vases, I would be compelled to discuss them in general terms, theoretically, and no faint shadow of knowledge would tempt me into stating as fact something which was not; nor would I be tempted to cite incomplete examples, such as the one you've just outlined.

Spike: So, it's better to write about things you know nothing about than things you know little about?

Rupert: In my view, it is, yes.

Spike: Fair enough. Let us move on to something else. The time has come, the interviewer said, to analyse the text. Give me your views on the first paragraph.

Rupert: There's not much I can say about the first, rather short, paragraph. It merely expresses, quite badly in fact, the view that the opinion given in the question has some element of veracity but that there are other, more substantive factors that have caused the alleged upsurge in the popularity of museums.

Spike: The essay begins in proper in the second paragraph, then?

Rupert: I think so; and I believe there are two points to be noted. Firstly, that the answer is vaguely sociological and secondly, that there begins here a mild form of euphuism which goes on to pervade the entire essay.

Spike: The euphuism is recognized and remarked upon, in her final comment, by your teacher.

Rupert: Yes, she remarked that there was generally a good use of language.

Spike: Was there, do you think?

Rupert: Yes, the language isn't bad. The first sentence of the second paragraph is rather long, as indeed are most others ...

Spike: Yet, despite its length, it boasts not one single fact.

Rupert: Don't you think that some of your readers might feel that you're making rather more out of this business of facts than it actually merits.

Spike: If they were to think that, they'd be entirely correct: I am. It is the nature of this work to make something out of nothing, by whatever means present themselves to my imagination. I make no apology for the apparent, and probably actual, inanity of the discussions: let those who like them read them and those who do not, turn elsewhere for their distractions.

Rupert: You can't say fairer than that, I suppose.

Spike: What about the opinion you put forward in that first sentence?

Rupert: It may well be valid; on the other hand, it may be invalid. Who knows? Certainly not me.

Spike: It's not an unreasonable proposition. In fact, I'd probably be inclined to argue in favour of it.

Rupert: You're very kind.

Spike: I assure you, that is not my intention.

Rupert: I see ... anyway, the next sentence contains an assertion that might well be factual. I state with convincing confidence that during the Victorian period the museum began its rise.

Spike: Are you saying that this may or may not be true?

Rupert: I am; though I have to say that I believe it is true on account of the fact that my teacher passed over it without comment.

Spike: She may have passed over it without comment because you stated it with 'convincing confidence'.

Rupert: That also remains a possibility.

Spike: Anyway, do go on with what you were saying.

Rupert: While writing the essay I simply did not know when the museum began its rise ...

Spike: So, you guessed, taking care to state your guess with ...

Rupert: ... convincing confidence, yes.

Spike: Why did you guess the Victorian period?

Rupert: For two reasons, really: firstly, I had a sneaking suspicion that it actually was the Victorian period - borne out by the age of many museum buildings; and secondly, Queen Victoria was on the throne for a sufficiently long period of time to give me a fairly good statistical chance of being correct.

Spike: Not only a guess then, but an educated one.

Rupert: Indeed.

Spike: What about all this 'old social order' business? Was there, indeed - is there, some political point being made here?

Rupert: Yes, of course there is; and a very valid one. I don't have any figures with me at the moment, but let me tell you this: museums are becoming less popular again, only marginally perhaps, but still less popular. Are we to believe that this is due to a decline in the techniques of presentation?

Spike: You tell me.

Rupert: No, we are to attribute this lamentable fact to the continuation in office of this present cut-throat Conservative government. Museums and other such places of interest are bound to become less popular as local councils are forced to cut grants to maintain more vital public services.

Spike: You blame the government then? But surely it was a Conservative government that allowed people to buy their own council houses and is it not they, therefore, who have largely contributed to the wider ownership of property.

Rupert: It all looks very well on the surface, I'll agree; but look beneath the surface and what do you find? A festering hive of capitalist maggots lying in wait for people to start missing their mortgage payments and then what?

Spike: Repossession, I imagine.

Rupert: Precisely. How many of the council houses that were sold to their occupiers in the boom years are now owned by the various building societies, companies and housing cartels?

Spike: I don't know.

Rupert: You wouldn't. Those are the figures you never see in their white papers and parliamentary reports. Houses which were built by the public trust for the benefit of the nation's citizens are now owned not by the people who live in them but by large, often foreign based, companies. Many of these houses lie empty while the financiers wait for the market to pick up.

Spike: And when it does?

Rupert: The houses will be sold for the profit of the directors and shareholders. Thus, those who already have homes will get wealthier and wealthier, while ever greater numbers of their fellow citizens will be condemned to live in one room bed-sits or sleep on the streets in cardboard boxes.

Spike: You paint a very gloomy picture, but nonetheless, paint well. I fear we have strayed rather too far from the intended subject to continue, though. Allow me to re-direct you, if I may, by turning your attention to the fifth paragraph of the essay.

Rupert: Of course.

Spike: You state that 'one other type of museum worthy of mention is the industrial museum', but then you go on to say that you have not visited any such places because you are not interested in them. To which, your teacher replied: 'Do not emphasize your own restricted interests! This shows a closed mind!!' How do you react to that?

Rupert: Without doubt, that particular paragraph is a piece of worthless padding which adds nothing to, and does in fact detract from, the essay. It would have been far better to omit it altogether. However, having said that, I must say that I do not agree with my teacher's comment.

Spike: Why not?

Rupert: It may not be wise to emphasize one's restricted interests, but it is unavoidable to have them.

Spike: Restricted interests, you mean?

Rupert: Of course. Everyone's interests are restricted; both by personal inclination and the not insignificant fact that there are only twenty-four hours in a day. Everyone's interests are either restricted or shallow; there is simply no third possibility.

Spike: Perhaps a fair point; and at that let us move on to the last paragraph - and your conclusion.

Rupert: I stand by the first sentence of the paragraph absolutely.

Spike: And the second?

Rupert: It provides, in my view, a rather startling example of what one can get away with in terms of incoherence by stringing a few 'posh' words together into a sentence.

Spike: In what way?

Rupert: A 'factor', in the context of the last sentence, can be defined and, I would argue, should be defined as 'a circumstance contributing to a result'. This being so, I see a faint resemblance between the last sentence and the almost proverbial sailing raft blown along by wind produced by an attached fan.

Spike: Are the laws of Newtonian physics, then, possibly analogous to those of dependence?

Rupert: They may in fact be one and the same.

Spike: Lastly, what do you make of your teacher's final comment?

Rupert: I think my teacher missed the point of the essay altogether.

Spike: In what way?

Rupert: What are the implications of the admonition 'Why not analyse the improvements made in scientific museums?'

Spike: You tell me.

Rupert: My teacher seems not to have understood the thrust of the essay at all. An analysis of the improvements made in scientific museums would have been completely irrelevant, as indeed would have an analysis of the improvements made in any museum. You see, I discounted the contention that improvements in the techniques of display and presentation were, or are, a major contributory factor in the upsurge in the popularity of museums: what purpose, then, would analysis of such improvements serve?

Spike: None whatever.

Rupert: Precisely. By suggesting such a course, my teacher appears to have ignored everything I said and assumed that the improvements in the techniques of display and presentation are the major contributory cause, which clearly they are not.

Spike: And what of the criticism that your essay was 'woolly' and based not upon facts but upon your opinions?

Rupert: I discount the comment completely. If the person or persons who set the essay question had required a so-called factually based essay, they would have said 'Comment upon and discuss the improvements in the techniques of display and presentation at museums', which clearly they did not do. I would argue that an essay based on facts was not required; what was required was what I wrote. Furthermore, I was right; I got a D for this essay and an A in the actual exam. If that is not a vindication of my approach, then what is?

Spike: I take your question to be rhetorical.

Rupert: It is.

Spike: Thank you for speaking to me; it has been a most enjoyable discussion.

Rupert: Thank you.

CHAPTER 11: MINORITY INTEREST VIEWING

Introduction

Following on from my theme in Chapters 4, 5 and 7, and resulting again from the same advert, I received one final piece representing this most fascinating genre.

The Interview: Part I

Spike: Excuse me, I'm looking for someone called Titus...

Titus: Spike, I presume.

Spike: You presume correctly.

Titus: Please, have a seat.

Spike: Thanks.

Titus: You want some coffee?

Spike: Sure.

Titus: Espresso? Cappuccino?

Spike: Espresso would be great.

Titus: Giovanni ... due espressi!

Spike: You speak Italian as well?

Titus: It comes from sitting around in Italian restaurants all day.

Spike: Sounds like a good life.

Titus: I've no complaints.

Spike: Anyway, thank you for agreeing to meet me; I know you must be very busy. I'll try to be as brief as possible.

Titus: Nonsense, you can take all day ... until five-thirty anyway; I have to give a lecture at six.

Spike: On what subject?

Titus: The theological basis of the papal inquisition of Pope Gregory IX.

Spike: Fascinating.

Titus: One of my pet curiosities.

Spike: I have to say, I was greatly surprised when I received your letter ... perhaps I should say letters. I'd never have imagined that so eminent a person would be interested in making a contribution to my book.

Titus: I only sent the letter on a whim actually; I never thought anything would come of it. I was surprised myself when you phoned me and asked for a rendezvous, especially in light of the distance you've had to travel in order to meet me. If you were going to use my name in the book I could perhaps understand your enthusiasm to interview me, but as you maintain that you only ever refer to your contributors by their first names, I must confess that I'm baffled.

Spike: Then be baffled no longer; I wanted to interview you because I found your letter, the one we're going to talk about - not the one you wrote to me ...

Titus: Of course.

Spike: ... because I found it astonishing. It goes far beyond the bounds of excess; it reminded me in fact of Escher's waterfall.

Titus: I'm tempted to ask you why; but perhaps I should wait a while until we're further into our discussion.

Spike: Thank you: it would be better to wait until later ... for reasons which I hope will become apparent.

Titus: Fair enough. Let me ask you something, though.

Spike: Sure.

Titus: What is your book about?

Spike: It's about pieces of school work.

Titus: What about them?

Spike: What they say, how they say it and what the answer to either or both of those questions means.

Titus: Remarkable ... and very unusual.

Spike: I'm glad you think so.

Titus: I could hardly think anything else; but will it be publishable?

Spike: Anything is publishable these days. The question is: will anyone buy it?

Titus: Only time will answer that question ... ah, the espresso is coming. Cigar?

Spike: Thanks ... thanks.

Titus: How do you wish to proceed then? Do you like to follow a set format?

Spike: Yes, generally. First of all, I'd like to ask you about the circumstances in which you wrote the letter.

Titus: But didn't I explain that in the letter I wrote to you?

Spike: Of course, but for the benefit of the reader ...

Titus: Sure, excuse me I was forgetting. I wrote the letter back in 1984 when my daughter was in her fourth year of High School. She came up to my study one night and confessed to me that she'd been neglecting her work for the first part of the term. To cut a long story short, she was going to be dropped into the lower English set if she didn't produce some reasonable written work.

Spike: So, you drafted this letter for her to copy and hand in?

Titus: That's about it: yes.

Spike: But isn't that terribly dishonest; especially in light of your position?

Titus: Yes, it is dishonest; but she is my daughter and I didn't want her self-esteem dented by being put in a lower set.

Spike: I suppose that's understandable; I'm not sure it's ethical but then ethics is really your domain.

Titus: Sometimes being a good father means acting in a slightly unethical manner. Besides, it's hardly comparable to covering for her if she'd just killed her boyfriend.

Spike: No ... I don't suppose it is. It's at about this point in my printing of the interviews that I like to insert the piece of work. Can you remember the question, by any chance?

Titus: Erm ... not off hand. Let me see though, I'm sure I could make something up from looking at the first paragraph ... yes, it's coming back to me now. It was something akin to: write a letter to 'The TV Times' expressing your concern that the recently launched Channel Four should attempt to meet the interests of minority groups.

Spike: That's fine; it's at this point then that I'll be printing the actual letter.

<u>The Letter.</u>

ADDRESS WITHHELD

The Editor,
'TV Times',
13-17 Fleet Street,
London,
CW 156.

1:2:84

Dear Sir,

I am writing to you concerning minority interest programmes on the fourth television channel. I think very few people today care about the European Reformation of the mid-16th Century and that therefore it is a minority interest subject.

On television these days there are hardly any programmes on the said subject and period. Although I have seen many interesting, entertaining and informative films, and other productions, on the English Reformation, during one of which Henry VIII quoted from the eighteenth chapter and sixteenth verse of the third book of Moses, commonly called Leviticus, "Thou shalt not uncover the nakedness of thy brother's wife", I have seen no such productions on the more general Reformation. **(BROTHER'S NAME WAS ARTHUR)** To my recollection I have only ever seen two films on the European Reformation, both of which were on the BBC I hasten to add. The two I watched were quite good. The most recent was called "The Last Valley", although I may be mistaken - it was a while ago. The film concerned a group of mercenary soldiers during the Thirty Years War. **(A FINE PRODUCTION!)** It was an excellent production, scenery and theme - well chosen, theme music and photography - both skilful and appropriate.

The second film I remember rather less vividly. It concerned the heretical, German, Augustinian monk, namely Martin Luther - of worthy reputation.

Well, I would just like to finish by saying that I think many people might enjoy watching such programmes on this the previously mentioned subject and furthermore I have every confidence efforts will be made on your part.

Yours sincerely,

A.A.

Mark and Teacher's Comment.

18/20   Very Good.

The Interview: Part II

Spike: I'd like to turn now to what you actually wrote in the letter. Before we do that though, I'd like to ask you if you're a gambling man.

Titus: Hmm ... what an unusual question: why do you ask?

Spike: You said that you wrote this letter to prevent your daughter from being dropped to a lower English set.

Titus: That's right.

Spike: But wasn't it a gamble?

Titus: In what way?

Spike: Don't you think, as a professional marker of written work, that this letter could quite easily have been awarded a far lower mark by, say, a less erm ... a less well-disposed marker?

Titus: Perhaps I should say that I was aware of the marker's disposition.

Spike: How?

Titus: By analysing my daughter's earlier work and the marks she received for it. There's an old saying: know thine enemy.

Spike: Not only are you a theologian and philosopher then, but also, it seems, a psychologist.

Titus: I shall not allow false modesty to influence my answer to that question.

Spike: Shall I take that as an affirmative response?

Titus: By all means.

Spike: Moving on now, to the actual content of the letter, I would like to say first of all that I found it absolutely astonishing.

Titus: Is that a complement?

Spike: It is, yes. The letter demonstrates the most remarkable manipulation of a question, and the person marking the answer to it, that I've so far witnessed.

Titus: In what way?

Spike: You were asked, or rather your daughter was asked, to write a letter about minority interest viewing on Channel Four. What you actually wrote about was coverage of the Reformation, and associated history, on British television; and in fact, not even only that - one whole paragraph is taken up by Henry VIII's grounds for his divorce of Catherine of Aragon, and even then not plainly.

Titus: And you find that commendable?

Spike: Indeed, I do. Not only did you turn the question around so that you could write about whatever took your fancy; but you also justified doing so by using extremely partisan logic.

Titus: I wouldn't dream of doing anything like that.

Spike: Perhaps you wouldn't ... now: but in 1984 you not only dreamed of doing it, you actually did it. Allow me to expand.

Titus: By all means.

Spike: In the first sentence, you state: 'I am writing to you concerning minority interest programmes on the fourth television channel.'

Titus: But isn't that fair enough?

Spike: Certainly; wholly justified by the question. But in the second sentence you write: 'I think very few people today care about the European Reformation of the mid-16th Century and that therefore it is a minority interest subject.'

Titus: So?

Spike: What you were actually saying is: (a) I don't like the question, (b) I'm not going to address it, except in a roundabout sort of way, (c) what I am going to write about is the European Reformation of the mid-16th Century, and (d) you can't knock any marks off for this, Mr. Examiner, because I've justified what I'm doing logically, i.e. not many people are interested in the European Reformation, therefore it's a minority interest subject, therefore I can write about it instead of writing about minority interest viewing in general. Is that, do you think, a fair assessment?

Titus: Mmm ... I suppose so. Go on.

Spike: So, your first sentence then, is rather misleading, is it not? Instead of saying 'I am writing to you concerning minority interest programmes on the fourth television channel' you should actually have said 'I am writing to you concerning the lack of programmes on the European Reformation on all four television channels'; is that not so?

Titus: Yes, it's so.

Spike: The next thing you say, 'On television these days there are hardly any programmes on the said subject and period', is quite true and probably a fair point; but what of the next, mammoth sentence, of no less than sixty-one words?

Titus: What of it?

Spike: 'Although I have seen many interesting, entertaining and informative films, and other productions, on the English Reformation - during one of which Henry VIII quoted from the eighteenth chapter and sixteenth verse of the third book of Moses, commonly called Leviticus, "Thou shalt not uncover the nakedness of thy brother's wife" - I have seen no such productions on the more general Reformation.' It's a beautiful sentence by the way, there's no doubt about that; but what bearing upon anything does the quotation from Leviticus have? What does it have to do with minority interest programmes?

Titus: Mmm ... it erm ... it doesn't have anything to do with minority interest programmes.

Spike: And that's precisely the point I'm trying to make. You string together a sixty-one word sentence that has no bearing on the matter in hand and how does the teacher react? By inserting a note in the margin asking why it's there? No: he ticks it and writes underneath: 'Brother's name was Arthur'! Now I have to ask you: what's going on?

Titus: Henry's brother was called Arthur, there can be little doubt about that.

Spike: But surely that's not the point?

Titus: No, it isn't. The point is this: by writing on a subject that appeals to an eccentric teacher, you can more or less write whatever you want - within the bounds of that subject. I don't want that to be taken as a criticism of the teacher, though; my daughter's English Master was a competent grammarian and even when confronted by work on a subject which interested him, never failed to deduct marks for slipshod punctuation and spelling.

Spike: You think the mark of eighteen out of twenty was justified then?

Titus: I do, yes. Work which is slightly unusual or off the beaten track should never be penalised on that basis. Anything which seeks to subvert monotony and ennui should be praised and exalted.

Spike: That's no doubt a perfectly valid point of view; but is the view that students should answer the question set and not make their own up, any less valid?

Titus: No, I don't think it is: the two views are equally valid. I prefer the latter: ingenuity should be rewarded with high marks.

Spike: Fair enough. Let's move on now to your recollections of the two films you had seen concerning the European Reformation.

Titus: Certainly.

Spike: You say in the letter that both films were on the BBC?

Titus: That's right; I believe they were.

Spike: Haven't you ever seen a film on the subject of the European Reformation on independent television?

Titus: Not to my recollection, no.

Spike: Is it your contention, then, that no such films have ever been televised by independent television?

Titus: No, I merely stated that I didn't recall ever having seen any.

Spike: I see. You wrote that "The Last Valley" was 'an excellent production'; your - I'm sorry - your daughter's teacher endorsed that view, describing it as 'a fine production'. What was so good about the film?

Titus: The best thing about it was undoubtedly that it was set during 'The Thirty Years War'.

Spike: You say that the film was set during the 'Thirty Years War'; but surely that didn't begin until 1618, exactly 101 years after Luther nailed his theses to the door of the Schlosskirche at Wittenberg. How then can you say that the film deals with the European Reformation?

Titus: Counter-Reformation would doubtless have been more accurate. Nevertheless, the point remains: the 'Thirty Years War' was a direct result of Luther's break with Rome. Please don't be pedantic and say that the recent unrest in Northern Ireland was as well; I'm sure you take my point.

Spike: I do, yes: it's a fair point. What about the other film you referred to? The one concerning the great man himself.

Titus: By 'great man' you no doubt mean Luther?

Spike: Of course.

Titus: Yes, that was also a good film.

126

Spike: Do you remember the title?

Titus: Erm ... not really, no.

Spike: Do you remember who was in it?

Titus: Yes, Stacy Keach played Luther.

Spike: Then I'm happy to tell you that the film was actually called 'Luther'.

Titus: How appropriate!

Spike: Indeed. A singularly poor production of the John Osborne play.

Titus: You have done your homework, haven't you?

Spike: Naturally.

Titus: Though I can't entirely agree with your assessment of the film.

Spike: In what way.

Titus: It worked far better on stage, there can be little doubt about that, but the film was characterised by some very fine acting, most notably from Keach himself as Luther.

Spike: I would suggest that Luther is an easy character to play.

Titus: I would beg to differ.

Spike: Then on that point we must disagree.

Titus: Fair enough.

Spike: That brings us, very sadly, to the end of your letter ...

Titus: And thus, to the end of our discussion?

Spike: I fear so.

Titus: Would you care for another espresso?

Spike: Thank you: I would.

THE END

... DEO GRATIAS ...